AUTHOR OF
ANNA'S TWO WARS

Mimi Paris

ONE MAN'S
REVENGE

A NOVEL

iUniverse, Inc.
New York   Bloomington

ONE MAN'S REVENGE

iUniverse books may be ordered through booksellers or by contacting:

iUniverse
1663 Liberty Drive
Bloomington, IN 47403
www.iuniverse.com
1-800-Authors (1-800-288-4677)

Because of the dynamic nature of the Internet, any Web addresses or links contained in this book may have changed since publication and may no longer be valid. The views expressed in this work are solely those of the author and do not necessarily reflect the views of the publisher, and the publisher hereby disclaims any responsibility for them.

ISBN: 978-1-4401-8550-2 (sc)
ISBN: 978-1-4401-8551-9 (ebook)

Printed in the United States of America

iUniverse rev. date: 01/28/2010

To purchase additional copies of this book contact the author at MPARIS3@aol.com.

Also by Mimi Paris

ANNA'S TWO WARS

Fleeing a forced labor camp in Nazi, Germany, Anna and Joseph become resistance fighters duringthe latter months of WWII. On their trail is barbaric Captain Stoltz, whose infatuation with Anna drives his furious search for the two escapees. Anna fights two wars—not only against the Nazis, but also a personal war to keep her lover, Joseph, from the grasp of the mysterious Ilsa. Events propel Anna and Joseph toward a surprising, suspenseful conclusion.

Man's inhumanity to man makes
countless thousands mourn.

Robert Burns

DEDICATION

Once again, to my husband, **Marvin**,
for his continued devotion,
faith in me,
and love of tuna fish sandwiches . . .
which have all helped see us through to publication.

THANKS

To my son, **Bob,** for keeping me on the "exciting" path.

To my daughter, **Jeryl,** for her caring advice.

To **Elliot,** who *knows publishing*—always there.

To **Phyllis,** my editor, "This is it! No more changes."

Finally to **Susan,** who spent a day in bed reading *ONE MAN'S REVENGE*—"couldn't put it down"—the greatest compliment.

1

Delray Beach, Florida

Nuri Mustafa looked up at the beautiful, young woman who just opened the door to his Adam & Eve Beauty Salon. She was every man's fantasy—tall with long, dark hair, huge breasts, and wearing a short, white dress that showed her off her great legs. There was something unusual about her coloring though—not a Florida tan.

Coming up to him, flashing an engaging smile, she said, "I've just moved to Boca and met a friend for breakfast nearby, who insisted my hair desperately needs a good shaping. I laughed, but I told her, 'Okay. After we finish eating, I'm going to the first beauty shop I see.' And here I am—you're it!"

"Glad to help you," Nuri said. "I will be through in a few minutes. Have a seat—help yourself to some coffee." A coffee maker, placed on a small glass table, held a full pot. She glanced at it, sat down on one of the white, leather chairs and poured herself a cup.

He returned to cutting Edith Hockhauser's hair while stealing a look at this beauty.

"You hurt me, Nuri!" His finely sharpened scissors were scratching her scalp.

"I am so sorry, Edith."

"Well, you can't be talking to that pretty lady and cutting my hair at the same time. You know how fine it is," she continued.

"Edith, I apologize again. Are you okay?"

"I'll live."

"It is all because I am so upset today, Edith. You must have noticed my entire staff is not in. I am doing everything myself." This is one damn thing that has never happened before, he thought.

"That's too bad. I'm sorry I snapped at you, Nuri. You know you're like a son to me. Oh, I almost forgot to thank you for taking on Jill as your shampoo girl. Isn't she sweet?"

"Yes, she . . ."

Without letting Nuri finish, Mrs. Hockhouser said. "That's why I recommended her. Jill's had problems, but her grandmother tells me that since she's been working here, she's changed and for the better."

"She is a hard worker . . . when she is here. But Jill is not here today."

"She probably has a good reason. Give her a chance, Nuri. You know her grandmother and I have been friends for years."

"I am not ready to fire her, Edith. Do not worry."

Nuri continued his cutting quickly while striving for another glimpse of the newcomer. He noticed that she had crossed her long, shapely legs and was sitting there, turning the pages of an old Vogue, sipping her coffee.

Mrs. Hockhouser went on about her recent cruise, and Nuri kept nodding, smiling, cutting minuscule strands of her hair, absorbing nothing of her conversation. Finished, he put the scissors down and took the blower in his hand, knowing it wouldn't be long until he could deal with the beauty having coffee. For a moment, he questioned himself. He was thirty, had a beautiful, Iraqi-born wife and an adorable baby girl; they meant everything to him. Owned his home and this shop. His parents were always supportive—after that car accident and to set him up in business. So why, with all this good fortune, was he going crazy over this stranger? The young woman looked up at that moment and their eyes met. He felt right then that his life would never be the same.

Finally, Mrs. Hockhouser headed for the desk with Nuri following closely. The heavy blast of a car horn meant Mr. Hockhouser was waiting, double-parked in front of the shop. Nuri was delighted. Shoving her American Express card at him, Nuri swiped it and returned it, gave Edith a light kiss on her wrinkled cheek and watched her dash out. He'd never been so relieved as when he saw her open the door of the car and drive away.

"Okay, Miss, now I can give you all my attention."

"I just want a little trim. I always keep my hair this length, no matter how hot it is."

Nuri gestured towards the back of the shop—the shampoo area. He allowed her to precede him. Her strut was tantalizing.

This man was also one who turned women's heads. Nuri was tall, just under two hundred pounds, most of it muscle. He had dark hair and eyes and nearly perfect features. He was wearing his usual uniform—a flattering, tight, black tee shirt and matching, designer jeans.

"Sorry, my shampoo girl did not show up today, so I am taking her place." Nuri watched as the young woman moved into the chair at the sink. He tucked a soft, terry towel around her neck and snapped on the deep green, plastic cape.

"Looks like it's just us," she said, glancing about.

"Relax then; let me introduce myself. I am Nuri Mustafa, owner, stylist and today, your shampoo-giver," he said and smiled. "As you can see, my receptionist, who is also my manicurist, is out as well."

Taking her hand from under the cape, she offered it to him. "I'm Laila Ibrahim, now living in Boca Raton, formerly of Miami Beach, born in the Middle East. Please call me Laila."

"Born in the Middle East, Laila?" Nuri asked, as he let the water run. "Where?"

"A hilly place in the northwestern part of Iraq, quite close to Syria. It's probably one you've never heard of—Sinjar."

"What? Sinjar? That is my town!"

"No, I can't believe it," she said.

"This is amazing!" Finishing the shampoo, he toweled her hair gently. Guiding Laila towards his chair, Nuri was still in shock. In the six years he had lived in the United States he had never met anyone from his hometown. He always thought how wonderful it would be. Laila certainly did not look familiar to him. Even if she had lived nearby, she was younger than he, and as a woman, their paths would never have crossed, not in the Iraq where he grew up.

"When did you come here?"

Looking like she, too, was thrilled to have met him, she said, "It's a long story, Nuri."

Glancing at his watch, he said, "I don't have another appointment until noon, and that is an hour away. I have cancelled all the manicures, but I kept a few of my stylist's clients for later. The only thing I must do today is meet with my landlord at six tonight. The store next door is available, and it would be great to expand. But why am I talking when I want so much to hear about you? Go on, by all means."

"Okay, Nuri. You're being very kind," she said, but she thought—he's hot!

Laila began, "I was promised to an Iraqi, a man my parents had chosen carefully, or so they thought; his parents approved of me. I never met him, but we exchanged photos, and he was quite handsome. I was eighteen, and he was thirty-two—running several businesses, the major one was a successful computer company here in the United States."

"It was said that he'd dated many Americans, but only wanted a Muslim woman for a wife. When the decision was made, my mother took me aside and said there was much I must learn. She taught me to cook almost every meal she knew, along with baking enough sweets to make any man happy. She wanted me to be entirely prepared for my responsibilities as a good, Muslim wife. I was a fast learner and anxious to go to the United States. There was little future for me at home in Iraq."

She paused for a moment. "About a year from the time we began our arrangements, I came here, married and studied hard to speak English well. People often tell me I have no accent— that I could pass as American. I know everything sounds fine but my husband took to beating me. Ramzi Ibrahim was an excellent businessman; we lived in a beautiful home on the shore in Miami Beach. He owned a spacious yacht where we had many parties. Ramzi enjoyed showing me off as the best of all the other women. But he was two-faced, as the Americans say. For those affairs he'd always insist that I dress seductively, which seemed to me sinful."

"To outsiders, it appeared that Ramzi was a wonderful, caring husband. He engaged excellent English tutors and personal body trainers for me. They were women. Ramzi said he didn't trust me with a man. My husband continuously hired and fired these people, as good as they were, for no just cause. He just didn't want me to maintain any possible friendship. He wanted my English and my body to be perfect, and for this, he paid them generously."

"If it is too difficult to go on, Laila, please do not."

"No, I feel better telling this to someone who understands."

She continued. "At one of our parties, I met a much older man, a wealthy Middle Easterner, Yasin Adeeb, a business connection of my husband's. I was almost twenty then and seriously thinking of suicide. I couldn't go back to my family in Iraq. You know how they feel about a woman obeying her husband. But I couldn't keep taking his abuse. Ramzi was insanely jealous and wrongly accused me of having affairs while he was away."

"Later in the evening, I noticed Yasin Adeeb looking at my heavily made-up left eye that Ramzi had bruised the night before, and then he continued staring at me until I felt his intensity. He looked from me to Ramzi, who didn't notice him, and then back to me. He nodded questioningly and looked for my response. Hesitantly, I nodded back. Obviously this was what he wanted. Strange as it was, I felt then that my days of living in fear were over, and perhaps a new life was starting for me. And it was so."

Nuri snipped away at a few split ends he'd found. Laila's hair was beautifully cut, obviously by an accomplished stylist. He hoped he'd do as well for her. At this point Nuri wasn't as focused as he should have been. Her story made him uneasy. "I feel terrible for you," he said softly to Laila.

She paused again, looked down, and then went on. "A few days later, after Ramzi didn't return from work and it was getting late, I received a phone call from Yasin Adeeb. I was nursing fresh bruises and was very depressed. Yasin told me not to phone my husband's office or anyone about Ramzi not coming home. He told me to get ready to leave the house as if I were going out for the evening—to pack nothing, to take no jewelry, but only what I would normally wear, and that a car would pick me up in an hour. He asked if that was all right with me, and said he'd explain everything later. I was to trust him. I agreed and was overwhelmed with joy. I would have taken any way out. I never thought I'd get away from Ramzi—alive. And so, eight years ago my life changed."

"What happened to your husband?"

"I didn't know when I left the house and got into the limo. Yasin told me that evening, and that I'll have to tell you another time. I must go. Didn't realize how long I've been here, my friend. I feel you now are my friend."

"Of course, Laila; I am," Nuri said as he touched her warmly on the shoulder.

Tears came to her eyes. "I knew I'd have to pay a lot for my freedom from Ramzi. I was unaware then that I'd never be able to see or contact my family in Iraq again."

"What a tragedy."

Though he was curious even after his comment, Nuri asked nothing further. Quickly completing Laila's blow-dry, he was glad there was still something to be done for her. His urge was to take her in his arms and kiss away the tears.

ॐ ॐ ॐ

Laila appeared anxious. She toyed with the cell phone in her dress pocket, wanting to get out of the shop, so she could call Yasin and let him know how well his plan had worked.

2

On leaving the salon, Laila walked quickly to her new, light blue, BMW convertible. The weather was its usual—sunny and burning hot but the top was down since that was the way Laila liked to drive. Her car was her second love. She also enjoyed the looks she got when she stopped for a light. Starting the engine, Laila drove for a few more blocks and then made a left turn into a quiet, residential street. Pulling over to the first available spot, she took out her cell phone and called Yasin. As soon as he picked up, she said quietly, yet excitedly, "It worked! He believed me—every word!"

"Good, Laila. Now come back. We will talk when you get here." Then she heard the finality of the click.

Early this morning when she'd been still sleeping, Yasin had kissed her softly and said, "Your job starts this morning, my darling. I received my phone call a few hours ago." He'd put the mug of fresh, hot coffee on the night table beside her. I think it would be best if you left for the salon about nine. You have more than enough time to ready yourself." Yasin certainly spoke more lovingly then than he sounded now, she thought.

Laila turned the key in the ignition. Perhaps she shouldn't have called; she should have waited until she returned. If Yasin were angry with her, he'd never show it. He'd always kept those things to himself. What came to her mind was, maybe he was saving everything up, and then one of these days he'd really let her have it.

She was about fifteen minutes from her new home: a condo apartment overlooking the ocean in Boca Raton. Situated on A1A, the view of the water could be seen from almost every room. A wrap-around balcony enveloped the apartment. Yasin said they'd be there for only a few months. She thought immediately . . . if not this place, the next one will be just as beautiful.

Laila laughed to herself. She was becoming a real princess for a woman, who for many years had shared one narrow bed with her sisters. Right then, she yearned for a nice long, relaxing bath with her new oils, and a drink beside her. In the short ride back, Laila's mind drifted to the story she'd told Nuri. Being born in Iraq was the only truth.

In record time, she was driving up to the entrance of her condo building, stopping when the valet approached. She smiled at the young man, stepped out quickly and headed for the elevator, once again thinking how luxurious the place was. Their apartment was elegant—done in white and beige, with deep colored accents in the Oriental rugs and paintings. The fresh roses were replaced immediately upon their demise.

As Laila reached her door, she felt strangely apprehensive. Why? Everything had gone well, she thought. But as she turned the key she had a feeling of dread. Or, it may have been her guilty conscience about the strange, sexual feelings Nuri aroused in her. She also found him so compassionate. This had never happened before in her many years of doing this kind of work.

Yasin stood behind the mahogany bar, holding a drink in his hand, having returned home a few minutes before her phone call. Laila walked to one of the huge, beige sofas, sank into its luxury, kicked off her heels and sighed. "Make me what you're drinking, Yasin. I feel drained. *Min Fadlak,* please!"

"Of course, my dear," he replied. "But, no Arabic, as I have said." He started mixing a Scotch Manhattan, as good a Rob Roy as any bartender in swinging South Beach. "Your accomplishments never cease to amaze me, my dear. I have taught you well." He walked over to Laila, handing the drink to her.

Yasin's gray curly hair was handsomely groomed, and he stood tall and straight—rather unusual for a man in his sixties. His dark eyes were alert, and his body was that of a disciplined boxer.

"It went so smoothly; I was amazed," Laila said, putting the glass to her lips, taking a generous sip and looking directly at Yasin, seated on the opposite sofa. "A perfect Manhattan, as usual," she said after the first taste, holding her glass up as a toast him. And then with intense fervor, she added, "This Nuri is so anxious to meet anyone who might have lived in the same town he came from that I practically convinced myself that everything I told him was true. I almost feel sorry for him."

As soon as she said that, Laila regretted her words. Yasin's face flushed, which was rare. He took a drink from his glass, then looked directly at her and said, "Let us not forget what is required of us; let us not let personal feelings take over. The work we have to do is difficult and far more important than the feelings of a beauty shop owner, particularly a man about whom you know nothing. There is more to this Nuri than what appears, and it is not good. I prefer that you do not concern yourself with him."

"Of course, Yasin. Whatever you say. I'm not forgetting our true purpose here. I'm just hot, tired and unnerved. Feel a headache starting, too. But, I know, once I relax for a little while, I'll be ready for whatever must be done next." She immediately drained what was left of her Manhattan and put the glass on the coffee table.

An uneasy silence permeated the room. Yasin sat there staring at Laila, and she at him, for several seconds until he spoke. "I think it may be necessary to once again go over the mission that you, Khaled and I have."

"That really isn't necessary, darling. As I said, I know why we're here and what we have to do."

"There are things I have not told you for your own benefit. Now, I want you to be aware of them."

"Of course."

"Our plan has two functions. We are to create an incident that will shock the world from its complacency. And in doing that, we will also involve Nuri Mustafa as the man responsible. His beauty shop staff, as you know, has a part to play too."

"Yasin, we've done many jobs in the past years that seemed to be more dangerous, and they've always been accomplished."

"I know my dear, but in this instance I was entirely against using these people, and I told that to our employer."

"And he still insisted?"

"Yes. When I first learned of the plan I said strongly that any one of them could contact the authorities, possibly terminating our more important objective. I was to inform the beauty shop staff to do all we ask or they will be responsible for accidents or deaths to themselves and their family members. They are my responsibility; yours is to handle Nuri Mustafa in an entirely different manner which you started today."

Laila looked out through the ceiling-to-floor doors that offered a clear, panoramic view of the ocean. Yasin went on. "Remember Laila, who we are. We work for the highest bidder. This time it is the group in Iraq. Next time? Who knows? Our reputation in the field is amazing, and we want to keep it that way. Our income is based on our successes."

"Yasin, I know all this."

"I understand you do, Laila, but I feel your compassion may be taking control of your common sense."

"It is not!" She got up, headed for the bar and quickly mixed another Manhattan. "Would you like me to freshen yours, Yasin?"

"No. . .thank you."

He resumed speaking as soon as she returned to the sofa. "It is our obligation, in the end, for an event that will jolt not only this country, but the world."

Laila stared into her glass.

The ring from Yasin's cell phone broke the tension in the room. "Khaled—I will have to get back to you in a few minutes, unless it cannot wait."

After hearing his personal assistant's reply, Yasin snapped the phone shut. There seemed to be no stopping him now. He didn't take his eyes off Laila, looking for her reaction. But her face was a blank. He paused only for a moment. Her eyes, too, were on him.

"In a short while our team of young men will arrive here," Yasin continued. "They are to be readied for the task ahead of them, though no definite date has been set. You are aware that they, too, are mercenaries, chosen carefully for this mission. They are not religious fanatics. In fact, they are not religious at all. Terrorism is their profession. They are working for one purpose, Laila, to obtain money so they can live the life we are living. I will stop here, my love. You have been well briefed on the rest."

"I have," Laila said softly.

"Let me assure you, my darling that I am proud of how well you did with this Nuri. I know it was difficult."

Yasin stood up, went to Laila, put his arms around her and pulled her up, holding her tightly against him. He kissed her passionately, then moved his lips along her neck and let his hands roam over her body. It was amazing, she thought, how physically attracted she remained to this man, no matter that he was aging; she still thrilled to his touch. Each time he took her in his arms, it was like the first time. Laila could feel his strength and was convinced that with his protection she would always be safe.

Laila felt his arousal, but this was not unusual. If he wanted her to lie down on the sofa now, she'd oblige with pleasure and perhaps that would eliminate Nuri from her mind. Yasin started serious business today so more than likely, he wouldn't continue, she thought.

They held each other for a few more seconds, and then he released her. Laila headed for the master bathroom. She undressed, dropped her clothes on the floor and ran the water, adding her aromatic oils. Her life, she thought, had changed drastically for the good because of Yasin. She'd promised herself from the start of their relationship that she would never displease him or refuse anything he asked of her. Her unusual feelings for Nuri were a complete surprise.

ഇന്ദ്ര ഇന്ദ്ര ഇന്ദ്ര

As Laila stepped into the warm, fragrant bath, she was unaware of Yasin staring at her through the open door with a troubled look on his face. It was hard for him to admit to himself that Laila could become a problem—a big one.

3

Baghdad, Iraq
Same day

Interior Minister, Rafiq al-Itaym, a brilliant strategist though half-crazed since the death of his daughter, Kamilah, stood behind the desk in his office. Seated opposite him was his nephew, Fakhari, employed as his secretary.

An hour before, the Interior Minister had been pacing back and forth, in what had once been a lavish bedroom in one of Saddam Hussein's palaces in central Baghdad, now al-Itaym's Office. Looking out at the stunning view of the Tigris River, the Interior Minister had whispered aloud, "Soon, soon, Kamilah."

Al-Itaym had been forced to give up his impressive workplace in the heart of Baghdad because of the dangers there. Explosives were often detonated in cars or office buildings around the area. The change bothered him little. Fakhari came with him and now worked at his desk in the adjoining room. Both inside and out, heavily armed government soldiers protected the mansion. There was far less chance of being targeted here.

A few moments ago, a knock at the door startled al-Itaym. His eyes started darting about the room. Deep set and dark, they reflected despair, hatred and rage. Knowing it was Fakhari, he'd answered, "Come in." By strong will, he'd presented a calm image.

"I have completed what you have asked of me this morning, Uncle. These documents are all ready for your signature."

"Thank you. Just put them down and I will take care of them later. But, Nephew, do you have a little time to spend with me?"

"Of course, Uncle." Fakhari placed the papers on the desk, pulled out the chair facing his uncle and sat down.

"How is my fine brother and all our family?"

"In good health. *Alhamdulillah.* Praise to God." Fakhari appeared to wait patiently for the real reason he was requested to stay but asked, "Do you mind if I smoke, Uncle?"

"Of course not, Fakhari," he said, and pushed a glass ashtray towards the young man. After his nephew lit his cigarette, the Interior Minister took a deep breath and said, "It is six years today that Kamilah, my youngest child, my only daughter, who I thought could do nothing wrong, was killed in that car crash."

"I was not aware of how important today was, Uncle. I am sorry."

"No need. When it happened, you were not yet living in Baghdad."

"It was terrible, Uncle. I remember how upset and saddened we all were over your loss."

The Interior Minister continued as if Fakhari had not spoken. "The car overturned and the driver was the only one found alive. Of course, he was taken to hospital, but the driver sustained only some minor injuries. The authorities' investigation took only a short time and they deemed it an unfortunate accident caused by heavy rains; I was able to obtain a copy of their report. But, from my own sources, I was made aware that the driver had been speeding on the curved, mountain road with which he was entirely unfamiliar. He knew nothing of Baghdad; his home was in Sinjar."

"That is unbelievable, Uncle…I mean it appears he was fully responsible."

"He was—and there was more. I also learned that although the driver was completely negligent, he was cleared of all responsibility after his hospital discharge. I am sure money changed hands. My daughter is dead and this man is alive and I feel that I could have saved her life."

"There was no way to do that, Uncle."

"Unfortunately, there was. Kamilah phoned me late in the afternoon of that fateful day. She asked if she could be permitted to stay at her friend Yasmin's house overnight. Kamilah insisted that it was better that they study together for an important examination scheduled for the following day. I told her that I preferred she be in her own home. But she pleaded successfully, and I finally agreed. Her last words to me were, 'Thank you Father. I will see you tomorrow.' But all I saw the next day was Kamilah's bloodied, broken body."

An uncomfortable silence followed until al-Itaym said, "The driver's family sent him to the United States to live with an older sister. But I have had that murderer watched all these years. Their eyes met for a moment with a knowing look. "I should have had the driver killed before he left for the United States," the Interior Minister said. "But killing the murderer outright, I felt was being too easy on him. It was not payment enough for Kamilah's death. I wanted to choose the method of his elimination and the time for the revenge.

The Interior Minister glanced out his window and said, "You can take your break now, Fakhari. Enjoy your tea, Nephew, and I thank you for listening to your old Uncle.

After Fakhari left, al-Itaym remained at his desk, pulled out his pen but did no signing. Instead his mind went to the time it had taken to get approval for his complex plan from those currently in power. He had secured the money from various foundations to implement it and consented to the rather unusual men for the job, choosing the best-known man for his leader. Along with the okay, he'd received words of admiration for his work. The goal of those powerful ones was systematic destruction of the United States. His goal was different. Although, he, too, had a strong enough hatred for The Great Satan to warrant creating this horrific incident, he also intended to tie his daughter's killer to the scheme. Strong evidence would be left to incriminate the man beyond a doubt. Arrest and imprisonment, he was sure, would follow and lead to the man's eventual death. In addition, his friends and family would be constantly harassed for possible terrorist activities. The bad publicity would result in most of the man's relatives being fired from their jobs or the loss of their businesses. They would penniless, ruined.

Nuri Mustafa, Kamilah's murderer, now a south Florida beauty parlor owner and an American citizen, would be taken from this earth and brought to the hell he deserved. Mustafa's wife would no longer have a husband, or his child, a father. This was the retribution the Interior Minister planned for the man who had taken his daughter's life. And along with that, the east coast of Florida would be in for a surprising disaster.

Al-Itaym reached into his desk drawer for a well-hidden, cellular telephone and made the call. I must focus, he thought. His contact in the United States, the one in charge of the mission, was waiting for the Interior Minister's signal to act. After some delay he heard the voice of Yasin Adeeb. No greetings were exchanged.

"Our plan is to start now; begin the telephone calls and all else required," he ordered.

And from thousands of miles away, now 4 AM in Boca Raton, Florida, came Yasin Adeeb's clear reply, "It will be as you say."

4

Strains of "I Wanna Be Your Man" suddenly blasted from Jill's cell phone. In the silence of early dawn, it had the same effect as a train going through her bedroom. She knocked her over-flowing ashtray off the night table in an effort to answer it quickly and not scare Grandma Florence.

When she said, "Hello," the foreign-accented voice asked, "Jill Rosen?"

"Yeah. Who are you? Do you know what the hell time it is?"

"Listen to what I say. If you do not, your dear grandmother will suffer a fatal accident."

"Are you some kind of nut? I know threatening creeps like you, plenty of them," and she hung up.

Immediately the phone rang again.

"Take me seriously, Jill. I mean everything I tell you. You are not to go into work today. You are to call the salon as soon as it opens and tell them that you are sick. I do not care what details you give them. You are good at lying, Jill; it should be easy for you."

"Why the hell should I do that?" she asked, her heartbeat quickening, feeling like she wanted to hang up again.

"Because I demand it! Be aware that I know everything about you. You are or were a drug user. I am aware of your stay

18

at a juvenile correctional facility for selling drugs, plus your arrest for shoplifting. These are certainly not fine character traits. But your life is now good. And if you want things to stay that way, you will obey me. Then, your grandmother will live."

"Who the fuck are you?" she asked again, hoping that she sounded tough, even though she was shaking.

"You do not need to know. One more thing: do not even think of calling the police. Doing that will end your grandmother's life, and it will affect your family in New York as well."

"Please, don't do anything to hurt them, please. I won't call the cops. I'll do anything you want."

"You are acting wisely, Jill. You can return to your work at the salon tomorrow. But, say nothing about this to anyone in the shop. You will hear from me soon with more orders."

A click ended the call. She held her phone, looking at it as if it had the answer to what had just happened. Damn it! Why did she grab her cell? She wondered. Oh yeah . . . she didn't want it to wake Grandma Florence. She had talked to this maniac, and here was Grandma anyway, pushing the door open and peering in.

"Jill, what happened? Who called at this crazy hour?"

"It's okay, Grandma. Sorry the phone woke you. It was a friend of mine who has a problem. I discussed it with her, and she's going to try to work it out. Don't worry, Grandma. Go back to sleep."

"Okay, honey. You, too."

As her bedroom door closed, Jill's mind wandered from one thing to another. This was the first job she had ever liked. Nuri was the best boss. The other women working there, Theresa and Helen, were so kind to her. She'd never missed a day even when she came home late from clubbing. Her new friends were terrific. She loved going to Maxie's Pub with them. And then Jill did something she hadn't done for a long time—she cried—convinced that wherever she went she brought grief.

ᔪᕮᑫ ᔪᕮᑫ ᔪᕮᑫ

A few months before, Jill had flown to Florida from the suburbs of Long Island to live with her seventy-six year old grandmother. She had been causing tremendous problems at home, and as much as her parents tried to help her, her behavior worsened. Jill's Grandma Florence, a widow for five years, had a two-bedroom condo in the Flagstone Creek development in Delray Beach. The stress the family was going through forced her father to phone and beg the older woman to let Jill come and stay with her for awhile.

"It would be a change of scene—she could make a new life—leave all her bad influences behind." Jill heard that part of the conversation when she picked up an extension at home. Her father's pleas must have done the job because before the end of the week, no matter how much opposition she gave them, Jill was packed—ready, but not wanting to leave New York.

Thoughts continued to run through her head. Why does this shit always happen to me? Who is this weirdo? Are his threats real? I know one thing—I'm not going to contact the police. Maybe he's only trying to scare me. But I can't take a chance; I won't go into work. Maybe this will be the only thing he'll ask . . . but what if it's not?

Jill lay back down, but couldn't go back to sleep. Time went by and finally around 9 o'clock, she lit a cigarette, picked up her phone and called the salon.

ᔪᕮᑫ ᔪᕮᑫ ᔪᕮᑫ

Yasin made two more phone calls within minutes of the first one. Theresa Giamonte, Nuri's only other hair stylist, was next. Helen Behar, the receptionist and manicurist, was last. He gave them the same instructions about not going to work that day. Theresa was threatened with the death of her fifteen-year old daughter, and Helen with the killing of her sick husband, should they notify the authorities or even speak of this to their co-workers. Disbelieving at first and then stunned and terrified, they both easily agreed to the foreign-sounding man's demands.

Theresa's husband had left her; he was wanted by the police. She was raising and supporting her daughter alone. She just sat up in her bed, stared straight ahead, a look of shock on her face. Helen's husband, once a strong and virile man, was in an advanced state of Alzheimer's disease. An aide came in when she left for work.

ಶುಃ ಶುಃ ಶುಃ

When Yasin Adeeb completed the last call, he glanced at his assistant, Khaled Ismael, a handsome, Arabic young man sitting across from him. "I believe I have succeeded in obtaining these women for our purposes. This first demand, as you know, was given simply to see if they would obey. I am concerned, though, about that young girl, Jill Rosen. She has a record of not listening to authority. The other women, Theresa Giamonte and particularly Helen Behar, the older one, appear too frightened to do anything."

"I will get Laila up around eight. She can be counted on, Khaled. She has done jobs like this successfully many times."

Khaled did not respond but instead took a large sip from his mug of strong, Columbian coffee. He'd been at Yasin's apartment since dawn. Although the adrenalin poured through his body after Yasin's summons to come, he realized he was fighting to stay awake. "It will work out; it always has, he said." But, this was not what Khaled really thought and he was reluctant to discuss it with Yasin. He had his doubts, but no actual proof. It was too late, anyway. The plan was underway.

ຮ⃝ CR   ຮ⃝ CR   ຮ⃝ CR

Back in Helen's house, as quickly as she had put the phone down, she picked it up again. With trembling hands and tears in her eyes, she called Information. "I need the number of the FBI office nearest to Delray Beach, Florida, and please hurry!"

Helen Behar's husband's family emigrated from Turkey. Her mother came to the United States as a child with parents who were Jewish immigrants from Morocco. The caller's voice bore an unmistakable Middle Eastern accent, an accent Helen heard constantly while growing up in the same home as her grandparents. Thoughts wouldn't stop coming: Could a Middle Eastern terrorist have made that phone call? But why would he pick on me? Am I going crazy?

That was when she felt compelled to contact more than just the police. Helen's hands trembled as she waited; she thought of hanging up but didn't.

Finally, she was given the number and with it in one shaky hand and her telephone in the other, Helen looked over at Dave. He was sleeping peacefully. What would she bring on herself and him if she made this call? Tears flooded Helen's eyes as she laid the slip of paper on her night table and replaced the phone in its cradle. Unknown to her, this would be the closest these men with big plans had come to being discovered.

Helen lay there quietly thinking. Depression covered her like a heavy blanket. The Alzheimer's her husband suffered from was going to kill her too, she thought, even if not in the same way. Adding to it, she had to deal with the strange man on the phone who knew all about Dave and threatened she'd be the cause of his death if she didn't obey. And he said there would be more demands. Helen didn't know if she could handle this alone but there was no one else. Her mind drifted off to the myriad of medications she had on the kitchen counter: Zoloft,

Valium, Ambien plus those ever-changing experimental drugs prescribed for Dave.

A shout from him ended her thinking. "Where's my dinner—you bitch! All you do is lay around all day. Look how long I'm waiting. What the hell is wrong with you?"

If Dave had been well, he would never have uttered those words, she knew, but what was important now was to calm him down.

"Dave—you had a nice dinner. Remember the fried fish fillets I made? You loved yours with the mashed potatoes. You were sleeping, honey," she said as she caressed his head and shoulders. After a few minutes, he relaxed and closed his eyes.

There was another choice, Helen told herself. What a cocktail she could make for the two of them. But not yet; the pills would always be there. She'd give it a little more time though it was sometimes a relief to know she had a way out.

Then again, she'd fought Dave's Alzheimer's from the minute of diagnosis—convinced him to go on the experimental drugs the doctor had advised. Accepting that there was no cure, she had hoped the meds would keep his condition from worsening. Yet he was becoming more forgetful and verbally abusive. Nothing was working though each day she tried to bring some quality to his life. What strength it takes, she thought. "But, I'm not giving up now because of that threatening bastard," she said aloud. Helen, tears brimming, looked again at what was once her intelligent, handsome and vibrant husband. A weaker woman couldn't handle this stress, she knew.

5

Yasin gazed out at the ocean and then back to the pool where a bevy of young women, some more beautiful than Laila, sat on lounges sipping their drinks. Their scanty bathing suits looked painted on their well-toned bodies. He got up, made himself another Manhattan and returned to his comfortable, overstuffed, leather armchair. He was enjoying the view but reminded himself there was more to think about than half-naked females.

Sucking on the maraschino cherry stem from his now empty glass, he thought about his immediate obligation, plus the beauty shop undertaking. He should never have accepted that job. Doctor Mohammed al-Hadi was his target. Until the past few months, al-Hadi had been on the staff of the American University in Beirut.

Yasin had been sitting with his superiors, some time ago, when he'd first heard the Professor's name mentioned. His mind went back to the conversation. "We have arranged to bring Doctor Mohammed al-Hadi, a Professor of Middle Eastern Studies, here to Florida Atlantic University in Boca Raton. His appointment will be for a year."

"I am sure you have good reason for this," Yasin remembered saying

"We do. And you, Yasin, and your associate will be in charge of observing and supplying whatever else we may need relative to this man."

"Of course."

"We will make sure you are generously compensated for this additional work. We can assure you that you will be more than satisfied."

It would have been extremely difficult for him to refuse the assignment . . . and the remuneration.

The group had continued to discuss al-Hadi. Yasin was told that everyone in the professor's family was a scholar, and it was not unusual for any of them to accept a professorship in other countries. Al-Hadi had been enlisted to discretely seek out students of Arabic descent, who appeared to be good candidates for their cause, and to recruit them, using the given strategy.

He remembered well one particular remark directed to him. "We know, Yasin, that in fighting a war, men are selected and trained for various purposes. You have your requirements and have been successful with those you have chosen. However, we, too, have ours, and we strongly believe that this professor will be an asset to us."

Yasin learned later that al-Hadi hadn't agreed initially, but threats to kill him plus his wife, children and grandchildren, who lived in Beirut, made him change his mind. Unfortunately, the professor's efforts at the university had been discovered. Yasin's plant at the college had informed him of this; there was indisputable proof. The fact that the professor was allowed to continue his teaching was because the FBI and Homeland Security, both on the case, thought he might lead them to others. Yasin had discussed this with his superiors and waited for their reaction.

It came this morning when he was called to a meeting. "We have decided to remove Professor Mohammed al-Hadi now, and the method will be left to you. Contact us when the job is completed."

Yasin had made the necessary phone calls to the salon staff, attended the meeting, and then listened to Laila speak about her pity for the beauty shop owner. His day so far had been most disturbing. Regardless, he believed his superior's decision was right. All individuals who pose a threat to one's plans should be removed if the organization was to remain effective. Laila's feelings for Nuri made him uneasy about the man, and about Laila as well.

Yasin picked up his cell phone from the table next to him and called Khaled. It was answered immediately. "Eight o'clock tonight at The Golden Veil, Khaled. Please make the reservation."

"Of course," Khaled replied.

"There are problems. But first a good dinner, and then we will talk."

"That is fine."

Both dropped the connection simultaneously.

Yasin decided to relax for a moment. He let his mind wander. It was pleasant to think of The Golden Veil, his favorite restaurant in Palm Beach. The dining area faced the water; the tables were covered in shiny, gold cloth, and only the best china, crystal and silver were used. The fresh flowers were tastefully arranged and in abundance. The elegant ambiance matched the food served. It was there that Yasin planned to allow himself some restorative time.

Gourmet, Middle Eastern dishes were always personally prepared for Yasin and his party by Chef Sammi. His concentration went back to the meal. Perhaps he'd have the pepper fish, a Lebanese dish. No, the red snapper would be best. It was like being back home when he ate their fish stuffed with green peppers and walnuts. And it was perfect with the lemony, tahini sauce. It was almost as delicious as feeling himself in Laila's body, he thought, as once again he scanned the beauties from his window.

Right after dinner though, the problem of the professor had to be discussed with Khaled and their course of action determined. His mind went to his associate.

Khaled Ismael was relatively young to have attained such an executive position. However, Yasin was in complete control of Khaled's life. Demands made of Khaled had always been completed to Yasin's satisfaction. Only the two of them knew where and how Khaled had come into Yasin's life.

That was ten years ago when Khaled was fourteen. He was ragged and dirty and sitting on the pavement of Al-Hashimi in downtown Amman, selling cigarettes and chewing gum. How he obtained the money to buy his wares was sadly etched on his face. Street-wise and tough in his manner, the boy appealed to Yasin. Walking through poor neighborhoods in the Middle East was one thing that was an obsession with him. Yasin thought how fortunate he was to have found Khaled on that trip to Jordan. He so reminded him of himself at that age.

Although it was risky, he'd lived like Khaled until he was twelve. No one would have guessed that looking at Yasin now. His mother had been a prostitute in Baghdad. His father was unknown to him. Yasin's life had changed when a group of politicians toured his area on a fact-finding mission. Like so many in that neighborhood, he was standing in a doorway watching their activities. Ultimately, one of the men approached him, "What do you do here?"

"Sell cigarettes and chewing gum when I can get them."

That answer, his smile and his charm, opened the door to the dramatic change in Yasin's life. Jafar Adeeb, childless, was one of the most influential politicians in the district. He was the man who stopped to speak to Yasin, eventually adopting him. Yasin soon enjoyed the education, polish and the love of parents he'd never thought possible. He gave little thought to the mother he'd left behind. He'd simply told her that he was leaving and picked up his few possessions. She'd stared at him blankly but made no move to stop him. Yasin always blamed her for the life he'd led before Jafar found him and never sought to contact her again.

Although it was so long ago, Yasin remembered Jafar's words exactly though he'd been extremely shocked then. "I have no sons or daughters, and I feel compelled to save you from the life you lead here. I have no intention of doing you any harm—only to give you an opportunity. Come to my home to live; you will be welcomed."

Yasin never forgot the look of joy on Jafar's face when he'd answered, "Yes, I will."

Another thing Yasin learned from the man, who had taken him into his family, was the loathing his wealthy, adoptive father had for America and the havoc he wanted to see brought to that country. Jafar was a non-observant Muslim, but passionate in his hatred for the United States.

"The United States is keeping the Zionists alive . . . keeping the Palestinians from their homeland. The Jews run the banks and the communication systems in America, and the country is dependent upon them. We must do something to stop them," he'd said many times.

That was years ago, Yasin thought. But after Jafar Adeeb's death, Yasin decided that he would do all he could to see that his adoptive father's wishes were accomplished. He'd found men and organizations that could and would help him. He'd found people with the same mindset as Jafar Adeeb. And even more, he'd found wealth in what he'd undertaken, particularly with the one facet of his group that made them completely unique.

₭℞   ₭℞   ₭℞

Jordan

When Yasin had first spotted Khaled selling cigarettes and chewing gum on the street, he found something familiar about the boy that he couldn't quite identify or place. This was not the first time he'd visited this section of Jordan. About fifteen years before he'd been in town with some friends. Feeling lonely on their last night, he'd left the hotel by himself and walked to what was considered a bad neighborhood. A woman approached him, offering sex. He remembered that night vividly because for weeks afterward he'd been fearful that he'd contracted a venereal disease. Fortunately, he hadn't.

"Where do you live?" He had asked the boy.

"With my mother, and he pointed to one of the decrepit buildings. She is sick now, has a bad cough that is getting worse. She is in bed all the time," he said.

Yasin had an important business appointment on the other side of town in an hour. He knew he must postpone it; he looked around for a phone and saw none. Khaled started to leave. Yasin took hold of his arm with a steady grip, took a bill out of his pocket, tore it in half and pressed it into Khaled's hand. "Stay here, and I'll be back in a few minutes. I have to make a phone call."

"There's a phone booth around the corner, near the pharmacy," Khaled said.

"Okay; thank you. You will receive the other half of this bill if you are here when I return. I just want to talk with you for a few more minutes."

Khaled watched the man walk off, noticing three dirty street kids following him closely. He debated with himself whether to stay or not. Business was not good. He knew his mother was dying, and he couldn't do a damn thing to save her. If he made some money, he'd be able to buy cough syrup from the herb woman. What did he have to lose? The man looked rich and promised him the other half of the bill if he waited. He decided he would. Khaled was sure those boys were up to something. Although they were only about ten years old, each one carried a box cutter. Most did in this poor area—Khaled as well.

He continued to watch the procession. The man appeared oblivious to his followers or believed they were no danger to him. Khaled thought he was a good man—seeing him give coins to the begging children who'd gathered around him. A man who came here, a stranger, and more so, a rich-looking one, could be robbed.

As the man passed a small dark alley, the young boys threw him down to the ground so he could no longer be seen. Khaled took off with the speed of an Olympic runner, made it to the alley and found one of the boys holding his box cutter against the man's throat. Upon seeing Khaled, they all ran off.

Helping Yasin up, Khaled asked, "Are you okay, Sir?"

"Fine . . . but a little surprised." Khaled watched as the man brushed himself off and smiled at him.

"You saved my life, young man. I can usually take care of myself, but I wasn't expecting an attack like that from children."

"We are all poor here, Sir, and some, even children, are more desperate than others."

"I see that. Thank you for your help. Now, I must make my phone call, and then we will talk more. I owe you much."

"You owe me nothing, Sir. All I did was show my face."

Yasin made no reply.

Khaled walked with him to the telephone booth, but stayed a respectful distance away.

After Yasin came out, he said, "I am glad you did not listen to me when I said to stay where you were." He took the other half of the bill from his jacket pocket and handed it to Khaled. "Can you go back, pack up your merchandise, and let me take you for a coffee? Do not think I want anything else from you. As I said before, I want only to talk."

Khaled smiled, knowing that was what they all said, but he was ready for anything that might come up. Now he was richer than he had been that morning. He'd met men like this one before, did what he had to do, and was always financially better off for it. He wasn't frightened. Knowing every inch of this hellhole, and prepared for every crook and murderer in it, Khaled was sure he could do away with this man in a minute, if necessary. But somehow he seemed different—believable. "Okay, let us talk."

Pointing to a shabby outdoor café down the block, Yasin said to him, "That place looks good." They headed there, took seats at one of the many empty tables and ordered their coffees. They both sat for a minute saying nothing. The coffees were placed before them soon. Yasin's hands were shaking as he held the tiny cup.

"*Maa ismak?* What is your name?"

"Khaled Ismael," came the reply.

"May I ask yours, *Sayyid,* Mister?"

"Of course; Yasin Adeeb." They shook hands somewhat clumsily. One had filthy hands with broken nails—the other, clean and handsomely manicured.

"Would you mind telling me a bit about yourself, Khaled?"

Deciding he would tell the man enough to keep him buying coffee and perhaps, get more money. He could do that for the rest of the day if needed. Khaled knew he'd done more to earn less, although he found it disturbing how Yasin Adeeb stared at him.

Yasin leaned back in his chair, poised to listen. He never took his eyes off the boy.

"I have lived all my life in this beautiful area."

Smiles appeared on both the men's faces.

"I am selling cigarettes and chewing gum to make money for my mother and me—to live—to eat—and to pay the rent. My mother told me that my father was killed one night by one of his so-called friends who had argued with him. The killer ran away and was never caught. That was long ago; I was just a baby, so I have no memory of him." Khaled smiled his handsome smile again and said, "What happened is not unusual in this neighborhood . . . but sometimes I do not believe her story."

"When my mother was well, she sold wheat cakes on the street. They were delicious. She fried and stuffed them with minced lamb. So many people knew how good they were and came to buy those cakes. My mother always took me with her. When I was older and there was not enough money to buy what she needed to make her cakes, she left me alone and did what she had to do. Now she is just too sick to do anything. So I had to take over."

Yasin continued listening intently, saying nothing, only occasionally sipping his coffee.

"Why do you want to know so much about me?"

Yasin looked perplexed. "I want to know about you because I think you may be my son."

6

As Laila stepped into her warm bath, Theresa Giamonte, Nuri's only other hairdresser, stepped into a shower to freshen herself after hours of crying. Her fifteen-year old daughter, Christy, was expected home soon from her school play rehearsal. Everything had been going well for the past few months, Theresa reflected. She'd finally found a fairly decent apartment in Delray Beach. Christy was enrolled in a good school, and her job at Nuri's salon was paying for all of it. This morning's phone call however, from that strange-sounding man threatening her and Christy, had brought the new life to an end. He knew so much about them. She kept remembering one of the frightening things he'd said: "I know that your husband, Mario, disappeared after he was involved in stealing thousands of dollars at the Toyota dealership where he worked."

ഔ ഔ ഔ

Mario had told Theresa that the Chinese immigrant he'd been trying to sell a car to was a perfect mark. She found out later from the dealership when they'd questioned her, exactly what Mario had said to the unsuspecting Mr. Yip: "Bring in the twenty thousand in cash that you told me you have at home. Then you can drive out in this Toyota Sequoia SUV with all the options, for half the price. In this country," he'd explained, "It's not unusual to do this for cash up front."

So now, Mario was a fugitive on the run, and she and her daughter were alone in the world with no one to help them, unless she counted Antoine. Thoughts entered her head continuously: Should she tell Antoine about the call? But . . . she didn't want him involved in this . . . whatever this was. It was enough that their relationship had gone from being the brother of her caring neighbor; to the intimacy they now shared. Theresa thought about how they met as she soaped her body for the second time.

Antoine Boyce was the brother of her next-door neighbor, Denise. He was single, good-looking and a mathmatics teacher at a middle school in Boynton Beach. He'd started out as just a friend, helping Christy with her math. He was terrific with her, and Christy was doing so much better. She felt that he was the kindest man she'd ever met.

Denise and her husband, James, had helped Theresa ever since she'd moved into the apartment. They were the first people she'd met. James had hung her chandelier, moved pieces of furniture that were heavy and insisted she call anytime she needed him. And when Denise cooked, Theresa often benefited with extras sent over for her. Knowing that Theresa was a single mother seemed to have made her become their cause. They also had a daughter, Olivia, Christy's age, and the girls had become close.

Theresa had met Antoine a few months earlier as the family was leaving their apartment as she was leaving hers. "Hey, Theresa you've got a chance now to meet my brother, Antoine—Antoine Boyce. You know, the guy I'm always bragging about."

"I always thought you must have a good reason," Theresa responded.

"That's a nice thing to say, young lady. My sister is special. I'm lucky to have her," he said as he gave Denise a hug.

"Okay, Antoine, she's for me to cuddle," James interrupted, smiling and giving Antoine a light punch on his shoulder.

"Nice to meet you, Antoine. Now, I have a face to match the name," Theresa said, offering her hand, surprised by the sexual heat she felt enter her body.

Taking her hand in his, Antoine looked directly into her eyes and said, "Theresa—that's a pretty name. The pleasure is all mine—and I mean it." He then gently released his clasp.

This had been the first, personal contact she'd ever had with a black family. Mario was completely racist and would never have allowed such a friendship.

ഇൻ ഇൻ ഇൻ

The sound of ringing filled Theresa with fear. Her heart beat rapidly. It couldn't be him again. She quickly shut off the shower, wrapped herself in the waiting towel, and ran for the phone. "Hel-lo?"

"Mom, what's wrong? You sound terrible."

"Nothing, Sweetie. I took a painkiller for my back. It makes me sound groggy."

"Called to tell you I'll be coming home later than I said. Our drama teacher told us we'd all have to go over our lines again after school. Olivia's Mom will pick us up when we're done."

"Fine, Christy."

"You sure you're okay, Mom?"

"I am. Don't worry."

"See you later then. Love you."

"Love you, too."

Hanging the wet towel over the curtain rod, Theresa finally made her decision. She'd have to follow all the demands of the stranger . . . at least for now. I'll try to calm down, she thought, have some tea and then call Nuri.

ಸಾಞ ಸಾಞ ಸಾಞ

A few miles away, Helen Levine, Nuri's part time receptionist and manicurist tried to come to terms with her situation. She'd been given the same instructions and warnings as Theresa and had already phoned Nuri with the only excuse that seemed believable. "Dave seems more agitated today and I must stay home with him. I'm sorry."

"It's okay," Nuri said. "Theresa and Jill should be in shortly; I'm surprised they're not here yet. We'll all pitch in. You've got enough to handle, Helen."

"Thanks, Nuri. You're so understanding."

"Hopefully, I will see you tomorrow."

"Of course."

7

Boca Raton and Palm Beach, Florida

When the valet drove up to them in Yasin's silver S500, no handsomer-looking couple could have been waiting. They looked like models for a Mercedes commercial. Laila, dressed in gold metallic pants that looked painted on, matching low-cut shirt and gold leather, high-heeled pumps. Yasin was handsomely groomed in a black silk open-necked shirt, black slacks and a gray blazer.

The ride from Boca to the Palm Beach restaurant was not long. They left in more than enough time for their eight o'clock reservation.

Yasin glanced for a split second at Laila as he headed down A1A, and then at the yachts docked on his left, ready to sail along the waterway. He looked tense, not ready for conversation. His business concerns seemed to be draining him, Laila thought. Even after the drinks and a warm, relaxing bath, she too was still uncomfortable. She knew it was about her discussion of Nuri with Yasin. True, he'd always treated her like a queen, she thought, since the day they met. Yet, she knew Yasin was a suspicious, intelligent, dangerous man, and she should have been more careful about what she told him.

"Did I mention that Khaled will be meeting us at the restaurant? He will probably   be there before we arrive," Yasin said.

"I don't remember, but I assumed he'd be there and . . . early—another one of his many good traits," Laila responded. Yasin glanced at her with a scowl but said nothing further.

Unexpectedly, he made a left from A1A in Lake Worth and drove over the Intracoastal bridge, heading west slowly. "Take a good look out of your window, Laila."

"At what?" Why are we going this way? she thought. Laila gazed out at the calm water, a yacht in the distance making its way towards them and the sun setting over the serene scene. The sky was still light blue in parts but now with peach, pink and lavender streams of color. It was beautiful and peaceful. "Can you tell me what I'm supposed to be looking for?" she asked.

Yasin turned into a public parking lot at the end of the bridge and then out of it, crossed over, and headed east. "I wanted you to see the 'before'. You'll see the 'after' soon enough."

"I don't understand."

"Not necessary right now, my dear".

As their drive resumed on A1A, Laila caught Yasin's eye in the rear view mirror, smiled and knew in a split second what he wanted. She put her hand on his thigh and moved it slowly to his groin. "Let's pull over for a few minutes, Yasin. I think you need to relax."

"It is amazing that you know just what I am thinking," he said and turned off A1A onto a small, dirt road, leading to a deserted home in the midst of being demolished. The car slithered under the overgrown foliage. Low palm fronds covered the Mercedes' roof and windshield, offering them perfect sanctuary.

Yasin slid his seat way back, as did Laila. Slipping her pants off below her hips, she bent over him, opening his zipper. She was amazed to feel how hard he was and looked up at him, her tongue wetting her lips as he guided her head down. With her mouth open and her tongue teasing, she felt Yasin's hand go from her head to her moist core. Yasin followed her moves exactly with his fingers. After a few passionate minutes, they let out sighs of pleasure and release.

After handing Laila his handkerchief, Yasin adjusted his pants. She wiped her mouth and straightened her outfit. He then took her in his arms tenderly and held her close, his body now completely relaxed. "Laila, you are everything I need."

"As you are to me, Darling."

Tears started forming in Laila's eyes, and only strong will power kept them from falling. She felt she was being tested for her loyalty, but she knew that she was completely devoted to Yasin and would always be. But, did he believe it to be true? she thought.

At that moment, lightning flashed and a blast of thunder followed shortly. Heavy rain pelted the car next as they exited their hide-away cautiously. Without taking his eyes off the road, Yasin took Laila's hand in his, kissed it, and said, "Good thing it is raining so hard, my dear; the car will be washed free of all the leaves and branches that were covering it."

She smiled, but had something else on her mind. It didn't relate to the weather or the car. I must get to the restaurant's ladies room for mouthwash. That thought stunned her. A few years ago, she could have stayed with the taste of Yasin in her mouth from night till morning. Was something happening to her? She knew he could still make her melt. Even his eyes could do it

For the remainder of the trip, Yasin kept his hand on hers. Laila began to think that she was needlessly concerned. She realized he had tremendous business pressures, and she also knew there was more ahead this evening than a delicious dinner. A long discussion between the men on current problems was not unusual. Most of the time her role was to sit patiently and not say a word.

As they pulled up to the valet at The Golden Veil, Laila looked at Yasin and said softly, "I need a few minutes."

"Of course, my dear. I understand. I will wait for you in the reception area."

Dinner that night was superb. As usual, Sammi, their renowned chef, fawned over Yasin. Khaled was already seated at the best table in the restaurant when the tuxedo-dressed maître d ushered them to it. Fashionably attired, Khaled wore a dark suit, light blue shirt and matching silk tie. He stood up as Laila approached the table; Yasin held the chair for her. If this wasn't so serious, it might be funny, she thought. I've got such polite, well-mannered murderers taking care of me.

Although chai, the Kurdish tea was served throughout the meal, the three finished two bottles of fine, French Chardonnay in a seemingly, short period of time. The Golden Veil was not a liquor or smoke-free restaurant that catered to the observant Muslim. Instead, it offered an excellent selection of wines and beers along with a full bar. Both Laila and Khaled had ordered roasted chicken preceded by tomato and okra soup. Rice, bread and a salad of chopped tomatoes and cucumbers were served and continuously replenished.

"I have had their pepper fish often, but each time I find it more delicious—tonight, especially," Yasin said. He smiled at them both, looking happy and satisfied, the opposite of his earlier demeanor. After they finished eating heavily-honeyed baklava pastries and drinking tea, Yasin said, "It is time to talk about our current problem."

They were silent as the waiter approached. Only he took care of them—no busboy was allowed to their table. The waiter carefully removed all the used dinnerware to a tray table. Then, brushed the cloth of crumbs, leaving new napkins, silverware, cups and a fresh pot of tea, which he poured for each of them. "Will that be all, Mr. Adeeb?" he asked, looking at Yasin.

"For now, this is fine. Thank you." Yasin answered.

As the waiter left the table, Khaled said, "Let us get back to what we call our problem. I can assure you the brilliant professor will not be one for long."

Laila was aware of the situation and had met the professor, but she was quiet. Knowing her place, she simply sipped her tea and looked out to the ocean, though in the darkness she could barely see it. In most Arabic circles, it would be unusual for her to even be present.

"I believe I have found the proper solution," Khaled said softly.

They were not apprehensive about speaking in this restaurant because the tables were comfortably spaced apart, and by this time, most of the other diners had left. The few that remained were seated far from them. The management never informed Yasin that closing time was near. The waiter knew to never approach until summoned. He and his party were always given every courtesy. Laila thought it was probably because of the tremendous amount of money spent for each meal—always paid in cash—or perhaps because his reputation preceded him.

Khaled looked about and then continued, "At first I considered two methods—a complete disappearance, which could cause unsuitable publicity, or a robbery gone wrong, resulting in the gentleman's death. However, both are not as safe for us as my third thought—his suicide. Yasin and Laila looked at Khaled quizzically.

He displayed his charming smile and said, "From the information on the professor that we have, I found that the man has a known, life-threatening heart condition and extremely high blood pressure. On top of that, he is here alone—thousands of miles away from his family. It is obvious he would be lonely and depressed. He could have convinced himself that his medical issues were worse than the results given him. Medications to control his heart and blood pressure, plus sleeping pills for his agitation, have been prescribed by his attending doctors.

"You think this is enough to make him suicidal, Khaled?"

"He has little choice. The professor was discovered because he was not careful enough in his screening of students for possible use. He knows an investigation has been started into his affairs by the authorities, even though he was not arrested. Knowing the consequences of his failure, I believe, is something of which he is quite aware."

After sipping his tea, Yasin said, "I am sure he is."

Laila took her eyes from the window and stared into her teacup. She was silent, but a lump formed in her throat. This reaction startled her. She was not a newcomer to talk of murder.

Khaled paused a moment and then said, "I propose to call him. We will arrange a meeting, and at that time I will speak about the matter. My advice to him will be the absolute necessity of his suicide. If he does not agree, I will inform him that his wife in Beirut will die, and for each week following that he remains alive, he will lose another member of his family. I think he will bow out without a whimper. The man has no money or ability to escape us, and he knows that we can arrange deaths in Beirut easily. He also understands how powerful we are. I will give him a week from the date of our conversation for his decision."

After pouring more tea into his cup, then looking only at Khaled, Yasin asked, "Do you have any concerns about your plan?"

"None at all. I will tell him that his death must be from an overdose of pills. He also must leave a convincing note, easily seen on the desk in his apartment. At first, it will be a tragic shock to the faculty and to his students, but it will soon quiet down. His family will grieve, and they will have to arrange the shipment of his body home. Once he is dead, we must not have any connection. This is all based on your approval, of course."

Yasin broke into a grin and slapped Khaled on the back.

Laila expected that. She thought about the news they had learned two years ago when the expensive, lengthy investigation of Khaled's birth was abandoned. Results from the sophisticated DNA tests both men took proved beyond a doubt that Khaled could not be Yasin's biological son. Oddly, this led to Yasin's increased affection for the young man. Still looking proudly at him, Yasin signaled their waiter. "Another bottle of that fine Chardonnay—we are celebrating."

Khaled looked pleased with himself, Laila thought. She felt sad but knew that she must appear the opposite. In the few times Laila and the professor had been together, she'd found him kind and modest. What a fine man and scholar the world would lose, when Khaled's plan was completed. In minutes, the waiter returned with the wine and goblets. He poured, and Laila brought the glass to her lips and toasted with them to their success. She smiled at each of the deadly, cunning men beside her, although her conscience rebelled against it.

ℰℭ ℰℭ ℰℭ

When they returned home, Laila was so high on what she'd drunk, that she leaned against the foyer wall and mumbled, "Yasin, I don't think I can make it to the bedroom," and with that, she started sinking to the floor. Yasin grabbed her at the waist to stop her collapse. He carried Laila to their bed and laid her down gently on the soft, satin sheets. Seeing her eyes closed and the innocent look on her young face, he realized he would always love her no matter what she said or did. Yasin removed her shoes gently, not touching anything else so as not to disturb Laila's sleep. As he raised the top sheet to cover her, his cell phone rang. He quickly took it from his pocket, flipped it open and left the room.

"Yes?"

"An appointment has been set for tomorrow night with our friend."

"A little late to phone him, was it not?"

"Now he knows it is important."

"I leave it to you, Khaled. You have never disappointed me before, and I do not expect you to now."

"It will be taken care of the way we discussed."

Yasin looked in on Laila who appeared to be in a deep sleep. After that, he showered, put on sweatpants and a tee shirt and sat behind the huge desk in his magnificently appointed office. Teak shelves and built-ins hid state-of-the-art computer equipment and storage space. A beautifully-woven Persian rug covered the floor, and huge windows offered a spectacular view. He slid open a door of the unit and took a bottle of spring water from the small, refrigerator.

Unlocking the deep, bottom drawer in his desk, he removed the folders he'd been working on the previous morning. Setting up a cell took time and energy. He'd further developed the plan given him, searched for the right men, investigated each and obtained the additional backing needed. The payment he was promised was astronomical. He'd performed many similar jobs before, but never was one giving him such cause for alarm from the start as this. Even though each problem was being met, Yasin still had a premonition of disaster involving Laila. He sat at his desk, looking at the papers before him and made a strong effort to push those thoughts from his mind . . . but it wasn't working.

8

A few days later, Yasin and Khaled sat in the breakfast room of Yasin's apartment sipping strong Turkish coffee. They were both reading news stories reported in the South Florida Sun-Sentinel and the Palm Beach Post respectively. Yasin's eyes were glued to page three of the Sentinel's local section. The headline over the column read, *Dr. Mohammed al-Hadi, FAU Professor Found Dead.*

The scene outside the window was of complete serenity—a sunlit day, frothy waves breaking on the shore, and a small sailboat bobbing on the water. The scene inside was quite different. A feeling of anxiety filled the room as the men appeared to absorb every word of the headline story.

"Quite a lengthy article," Yasin said. *Two deputies from the Boca Raton Sheriff's Office, who were called by the school to check on him, found the professor dead at his desk. He had not shown up for any of his classes or informed anyone that he was ill; his phone had remained unanswered.*

"Khaled, if they say the professor was surrounded by empty vials of prescribed medication and a suicide note, why are they claiming an investigation into the probable suicide is on-going? The man killed himself. How more obvious can it be? I am sure the suicide note was convincing even though they will not release its contents. Americans are difficult to understand. This troubles me."

"It will all resolve itself. The professor was much loved by students and faculty. I heard he made Middle Eastern History come alive. They cannot write him off too quickly. It is all procedure and paperwork. One thing the man was, and that was honorable to the end."

"It says in the Post that one of his sons is coming to the United Sates to accompany the body back to Beirut for burial. That will be the end of it, Yasin. I assure you."

It was then that Laila, dressed in a dark green, satin robe that matched her eyes, walked in unnoticed. As she reached for a mug and poured the hot coffee, she asked, "Bad news, gentlemen? You both look like someone died."

"Someone did," Yasin replied.

"Oh," she said softly, knowing never to ask whom it was. She simply turned and walked back to their bedroom in her high-heeled, satin mules.

Silence followed her leaving. The men simply looked at each other gravely for a moment and then resumed their reading.

9

Delray Beach and Boca Raton, Florida

"You're not doing it right, Nuri!" Edith Hockhouser shouted. "You know I like my hair teased higher in the front. What's with you lately?"

"I am sorry, Edith. I guess I was just daydreaming."

"Well, don't daydream when you're combing me out," she said and rolled her eyes.

Nuri continued silently, but the intense aroma of the coconut rinse was making him nauseous. His mind was flashing: Jill shouldn't be using that much conditioner. With Edith's hair, or lack of it, a teaspoonful was overdoing it. I have to focus. What the hell am I doing? I cannot think of anything but Laila. It has been a week since she came in, and I still feel so jumpy. All I see are her eyes, and her body. I want her more than anyone or anything I have ever wanted in my life.

As Theresa Giamonte brushed against Nuri walking to meet her next client, Nuri attempted to give her a playful hug as he said, "How about a smile for your boss, gorgeous?" Theresa continued walking right past him, looking dazed.

What is going on here? Nuri thought. Since Laila walked in, I am no longer the person I was. Theresa is so quiet and depressed-looking; I just cannot reach her. Jill is not the same girl I hired either. She snaps at me and at anyone else who speaks to her, and Helen cries and wipes her eyes constantly.

It is probably a coincidence, but strange. At that moment the phone rang, jarring Nuri from further thinking.

"It's for you, Nuri," Helen said, reaching for a tissue.

He took the phone, placed it to his ear and heard those beautiful words: "Nuri—it's Laila."

His face lit up and his eyes sparkled. It is Laila! It is Laila, he kept telling himself. "How are you?"

"Fine. I'm not calling for another appointment. The cut is really great though."

Nuri didn't care why she was calling. Just to hear her sultry voice made him hard. "Glad to hear from you, Laila, whatever the reason."

Though his back was turned to her, he could feel Edith Hockhouser's eyes boring into him. He covered the speaker with his hand and said, "Be right with you, Edith. Important phone call!"

"It always is when I'm here," Mrs. Hockhouser muttered.

"Well, Nuri, you'll be happy to hear this. I spoke with my fiancé about you and how you want to expand your salon. He's always looking for new business ventures. You did say that you'd like to expand your shop. Right?"

"Would I!"

"And I'd like to help a fellow countryman."

Nuri couldn't believe his luck. Laila had called. His wish had come true, and now there was a chance he could have the salon he really wanted.

"My fiancé would like to meet you."

"Sure, anytime." What am I saying? He thought. It cannot be any time, but I will adjust my schedule if necessary.

He noticed Helen looking at him and he turned away from her. Now he was facing Edith Hockhouser, and she shouted, "What's going on, Nuri? Can't you talk on the phone later?"

"I will be with you in a second."

"Nuri, I'm sorry if I'm calling at a busy time."

"No, it is fine."

"How about tomorrow night around eight at our apartment? I know you're not open late in the evenings, and we don't want to cut into your day."

"That is fine. I just need your address and directions."

"Why not take my number now and call me when you're not busy."

As Nuri started writing, his hand shook. "Laila, I will get back to you as soon as I can." He dropped the phone onto its cradle on Helen's desk just as she reached for another tissue.

"Allergies. Don't worry about me," she explained.

"Hate to see you looking so uncomfortable, Helen," he said and hurriedly ran back to Edith, who looked like she wanted to kill him.

"What's gotten into you, Nuri? The whole place here is going crazy! Helen is crying all the time."

"It is her allergies."

"It's not her allergies. I know allergies. Jill is getting snotty to me who got her this job, and Theresa looks like she's sleepwalking. She doesn't talk. She didn't even say, hello, to me. And, you, Nuri, I still can't figure you out. Enough already! Mel will be here in a few minutes, and I'll be glad to get out of this place."

"Come on, Edith, who else can make you look so beautiful?"

The smile she gave Nuri cleared the air a bit. He removed her cape carefully and helped her from the chair. Maybe things will be changing now for the good, Nuri thought, until he heard a crash from the back. It was Jill who dropped something on the tile floor. Liquid and glass shards were everywhere. "Shit!" Jill yelled. "I can't take this anymore! I can't!"

Theresa ran over to Jill and hugged her. "It's an accident, Honey. I'll help you clean up."

"It's not that, Theresa. It's everything!"

"What the hell happened?" Nuri asked as he dashed to the back of the shop and saw Theresa and Jill surrounded by broken glass and gooey lotion, expelling the sweet aroma of aloe and lilies—which now overwhelmed the heavy coconut.

"Sorry, I dropped a jar of Adam & Eve Miracle Body Lotion."

Normally, Nuri would be counting the dollar loss and reprimanding Jill. But after receiving Laila's call, his world remained too bright to do that.

ഇൗൽ   ഇൗൽ   ഇൗൽ

As Laila closed her cell phone, her face paled. She quickly smiled at Yasin and said, "Be assured, he's hooked. He'll call back soon. And if he has to crawl here, he'll make it."

"I am not that concerned, my dear girl. I knew we would entice him. As for the rest of the employees in that shop, they understand full well that they must cooperate or they and their families will suffer. But from what you have said, we might need a little more leverage on this Nuri."

Sitting across from each other in their elegant living room, they watched the heavy, all-day rain pelting the beach area, the sky almost as dark as night. Usually the expansive water-view, even when dismal, brought calm to those who could look upon the ocean. But on this day, it wasn't working for either of them.

"What concerns me is you, Laila. You and I are one complete being. You know that. We both fulfill each other. Am I right, my darling?"

"Of course," she answered, continuing to stare out the window.

"I must call upon you once again with regard to this Nuri. I want to make sure that he will never speak of what we have planned with anyone. At some point, he will be made aware of it, but strong evidence will be planted pointing to his involvement. Even with his life at stake, he will not talk because of the material we will possess. Whether he admits he is involved or not, makes no difference. He is the one who will be arrested and charged. Khaled and I have ready all that is necessary. We have been working some time on this part of the job."

"I didn't realize this was so complex, Yasin," Laila said.

"It is, and you will have to do what you have done a few times before. I know full well how distasteful you find it. But there is no other way. I am going to observe his interest in you when we meet. Should it be of the type I imagine, you will have to initiate an affair and see it through to have the photos. This type of incrimination has proven to be effective in the past, and we will need it now."

Laila didn't respond.

"Come my dear," Yasin continued, "It is not the worst thing in the world. Do as I said before, pretend you are an actress in a film. It is all acting. Love, I know you have with me. Now, cheer up. Why not drive down to that new boutique that opened in town and see if they have something you like?"

Laila stood up slowly, glared at Yasin, but still said nothing.

10

Delray Beach and Boca Raton, Florida

Nuri's right hand didn't stop tapping the wheel as he drove his ten-year old Honda down A1A. It was only a few miles from his salon to Laila's condo, but he couldn't get there fast enough. I better slow down, he thought. All I need to do is get pulled over. Nuri glanced at the water—the inlet on his right, and the huge yachts that were docked there. This was the life, and maybe now he'd get his chance.

As he pulled up to the curved entrance of a most luxurious, condo building, he noticed the valet heading his way. Should have expected that, he thought. He was embarrassed about his car. Once money started rolling in, he promised himself a new Caddy or maybe a BMW convertible. Where were all these plans coming from? He asked himself. No deal has been made yet.

"Check in with the Concierge, Sir," the valet said. As soon as Nuri got out of his car, the attendant got in and drove off to the parking garage. Pocketing the ticket given him, he walked into the building to the desk marked, *Concierge*. The security here wasn't the laughable kind usually found in Florida's gated communities. Sharply dressed in a uniform fit for a general, this young man looked like he could have been a former lineman for the Chicago Bears.

When Nuri gave Laila's name and apartment number, and then his name, he was questioned, "Are you expected, sir?"

"Yes."

After checking his list, the man asked him for a picture I.D., glanced at it, thanked him, and motioned to a nearby elevator. Nuri pressed the number. When the door opened there was Laila, waiting, even lovelier than he remembered. She looked taller in her sky-high, black pumps, black silk Capri pants and matching, v-necked top. From a chain around her neck hung a huge, gold-crowned, pear-shaped ruby.

"Come in, Nuri. Welcome to our home."

His palms were moist when he shook her hand, and he felt as if he were dreaming. What had this woman done to him? "Glad to see you again, Laila," he mumbled.

As Nuri walked into the dimly-lit living room, he was struck by the setting—the windows facing the ocean, the beautiful decor of the room—tasteful, yet comfortable. And more importantly, there was Laila's fiancé or partner or whatever she called him. Nuri took in the man's good looks as he came over to meet him.

"Yasin Adeeb," he said, offering his hand. "Please call me Yasin. I feel as if I know you, Nuri. You made quite a good impression on Laila. She was surprised and delighted that you came from her town. Sit down; make yourself comfortable."

Nuri headed for a huge club chair and blessed the fact that it faced Laila. He couldn't take his eyes off her. He compelled himself to turn his gaze to Yasin, whom he noticed was watching his every move. "Thank you so much for having me."

Yasin smiled and said, "It is really my home and office. I set up the den to accommodate my business. Would you like some coffee, Nuri? We have delicious baklava to tempt you, too. Or perhaps you would like something stronger: Scotch, rye, vodka, wine—whatever you prefer. Laila will be delighted to get it for you. Right, my darling?"

"My pleasure."

Nuri stared at the narrow table across the room, where coffee and small cakes were beautifully displayed. The delicious-looking, honey/nut pastries were set on a crystal platter. The coffee stood by in a silver urn. He glanced at the bar and the shelves on the wall behind it, noting the best in liquors and wines.

"I will have coffee—that will be fine."

Laila rose from the sofa, walked to the urn and poured the coffee gracefully, into a fine china cup. Turning to Nuri, she asked, "Cream, sugar?"

"No, thank you. I drink it black."

Two sets of eyes stared at her body as she placed the cup, saucer and napkin on a small table next to Nuri and walked back to the sofa.

Yasin was the first to speak. "I can assure you, Nuri, we won't be keeping you long. We know you have probably had a hard day. But I have to explain some things to you. I represent a conglomerate. They have entrusted me to find good, stable ventures in which to invest. For the past several years, through proper investigation and some intuition, I have led them to many businesses in which great amounts of money were made."

"I guess my beauty shop is a little small for your backing,"

Laila continued to sit quietly in her chair, observing the two men.

"Nuri, no venture is too small. If it meets the criteria set, then there will be a deal. Yasin drained the remainder of what looked like Scotch in his heavy crystal glass and continued. "I understand you want to extend your shop by absorbing the vacated premises next to you."

"That is right," Nuri said, taking a sip of coffee.

Yasin knew all about the cleaning store going out of business, as he'd made it happen. "I will need to have my accountant check your books and my architect examine the next-door premises and find out if it is suitable for the renovations. I must also learn approximately what the costs will be."

"Yasin, I have clean books; you will find everything in order. One of my employees, Helen, does my bookkeeping as well as her other work, and she is excellent. She accounts for every cash intake, every check received, every invoice paid out. I do not know what I would do without her." And for a moment, Nuri's thoughts went back to Helen's continuous tears. I must think of only myself now, he said to himself, and he quickly put Helen out of his mind.

"We really do a good business, but expanding would be a most important next step. I have always wanted to include a day spa because that is where the money is. Delray Beach is on the move. There are new condos going up, and the new restaurants on Atlantic Avenue are thriving. It has become the South Beach of this area. The over-forty crowd is flocking to it. And they are the ones who make great customers—repeat customers. This could be the first of a chain!"

"I admire your confidence and enthusiasm, Nuri. What if I come down on Sunday with some of my people—just to give it a look?"

"Great! I can meet you there around . . . around two in the afternoon. Okay?"

"Good."

"Sorry I cannot make it earlier. I must spend some of my day off with my wife and daughter."

"You are a good person, Nuri. I can see that . . . a family man."

"Well, I try," he said, regretting he'd mentioned anything about his family in front of Laila. He'd noticed, out of the corner of his eye that she'd picked up her head at that remark.

"I told Yasin that you were someone he'd like," she said in her low voice.

"Nuri, we will leave further discussion for Sunday."

"Okay," he quickly replied.

Yasin and Nuri stood, and Laila got up and walked over to Nuri. "This may be the beginning of a new and finer life for you," she said, offering her hand once again.

Nuri held it for perhaps a few seconds longer than he should have. He noticed Yasin observing the gesture. He then shook Yasin's proffered hand firmly and said, "Well, good night, and thank you both again."

"No, young man, you are the one who will enrich us all, hopefully," Yasin responded, giving Nuri an affectionate pat on the back and a warm smile.

As soon as the door closed behind him, Nuri wanted to scream, "Yesss!" and give some high five's. He had so much emotion pent up. As the elevator took him down, all he could think of was how his luck had changed . . . and for the good! He knew one thing he must do—he had to give up his desire for Laila. It would not be easy, but there was too much at stake. Plus, Yasin was aware of it.

As the elevator door opened to the lobby for Nuri, back in the apartment Yasin was speaking softly to Laila. They were both seated on the sofa. He put his arm around her and drew her slowly to him. "You know, my darling, he wants you—wants you terribly; I saw it all. I need him to incriminate himself. You will have to satisfy his craving. It will be a one-time thing. We can arrange it for next week. It does not take long to set up the camera. More young men will be flying in, and I need to start them working as soon as possible. You are aware of that?"

"Yes, of course, Yasin. You know I'll do what has to be done," her voice cracking when she spoke, tears flowing down her cheeks. She rested her chin on Yasin's broad shoulder—her arms around him, her face avoiding his.

11

Augie Costellano knocked at the door of Room 107 of the seedy Sunset Motel in what was known as *Shanty Town* in Las Vegas. He was tall, dark-haired and getting increasingly annoyed as he rapped louder. Finally the door opened a crack, and there was Mario Giamonte with a shocked look on his face.

"What the hell are you doin' here, Augie?" Mario asked, as he pulled the door open.

The Union Pacific train behind the motel passed at that moment, and Augie had to shout. "I flew in for some business for Richie Di."

"Come on in, you bastard," Mario said, giving Augie a bear hug, which was hesitantly returned. "Sit down . . . let me hear what's going on in Florida."

Augie looked around the dreary room, darkened with closed draperies, the only light coming from a dim lamp on a bedside table. It was just four-thirty in the afternoon, and heavy as he was, Mario looked handsomely well groomed—like he was ready for some nightlife. He wore an open, beige silk shirt and matching pants, plus a few heavy, gold chains around his neck. The room reeked of cologne.

"How'd you find out where I was?" Mario asked.

"Richie Di clued me in—he knew how close we were. He told me you were doin' some jobs for him, when he needs

57

you. And he said not to try phonin'—that you don' want any calls—so I figured I'd just try and see if I could find you in. Don' mention nothin' to Richie though."

Two worn, seventies-style, green leatherette chairs stood on both sides of a chipped, wooden table. Mario opened the bottom drawer of his dresser and took out a bottle of Seagram's VO. He then headed for the bathroom and brought back two glasses. "Listen, I never tell Richie nothin' personal. Anyways, it's good to see you, Augie. I really miss the guys. Hey, you wan' some ice? There's an ice machine at the other end of the corridor. I'll go and get some."

"No, don't bother. Remember? I drink it neat."

Mario poured the drinks. "*Salute!*" they both said, and clinked their glasses. Putting the bottle on the table, the men finally sat down and were quiet for a moment. Mario broke the silence first, "There's gotta be somethin' special you wan' to tell me, ain't there, Augie?"

"You're right," Augie replied, "It's because we go back so long, fella. Listen, we were given' and gettin' the shit kicked out of us in every school we were in."

"Yeah, those Bronx days were somethin', but I don' think you came to see me to talk about those fuckin' times."

"You're right, Mario. I guess you're really watchin' your step now with the cops breathin' down your neck. You know I had some shit happen to me years ago. Only they got me, and I did my time. I don't want to talk about that neither. But I understand where you're comin' from."

They both took a swig of their drinks; then Augie said, "It's about your daughter and your wife."

"So tell me," Mario said, refilling his glass.

"You know my daughter, Georgiana, and your Christy are good friends. They confide in each other. Georgiana feels so bad for Christy; she couldn't hold it in, so she tells my wife. Now you know Rosie, she goes and tells me. And that's why I'm here."

"You're talkin' in circles, Augie. What the fuck is goin' on?"

"It's your wife—looks like she's depressed. At least that's what your daughter is tellin' mine. It's been goin' on for a couple of weeks. She says that Theresa is cryin' all the time, and that she just goes to work and comes back like a zombie. Christy told my Georgiana that she keeps askin' her mother why she's feelin' like this. But Theresa says that she's not feelin' well—her back—and Christy should ignore her, and she'll be better soon. Christy don't think so."

"What's with that bitch?" Mario shouted, banging his empty glass on the table. "What is she on, drugs? No, not Theresa," he said, almost to himself. "I know I ran away from them, Augie, and they're strugglin', but she made me do it—my naggin' wife. I love my kid, but it was impossible to stay. She was always after me about not stayin' at a job long enough and that she was exhausted from standin' on her feet all day, workin' at the beauty parlor, and then doin' all the work at home. Claimed I never helped her—that she was carryin' all of us. Theresa pushed me over the top!"

"I know what you're sayin', Mario."

"Listen, when I was sellin' at the dealership and saw a way to take all that dough for the car this Chink was buyin', I knew that was my escape—so I went for it. And that Chink probably got his dough from a sweat shop where he was workin' women like animals."

"You're probably right."

Mario didn't comment on Augie's remark. He went right on as if Augie hadn't spoken. "Well, you can guess what happened next. When I got to Vegas, I gambled most of it away—kept enough so I could just get by. Then I heard about Richie Di bein' down here, contacted him, and it's been great that he's got work for me. I just gotta keep fit to make sure I can do his jobs. Don' get me wrong; the pay is good, and it's been some help.

Only now, I'm workin' on somethin' better. I was happy about it until you walked in with this news. I got no luck."

"Mario, I'm sorry, but that's not the only thing that's got me worried. Theresa's livin' in this apartment complex in Delray Beach, workin' nearby in a pretty good beauty shop, Adam and Eve, owned by some young Arab. But, it seems she's been datin' some guy—a brother of one of her neighbors. I found out a little about him."

"You mean that whore's got herself a boyfriend? I'll kill her!" Then Mario paused for a moment, refilled his glass, and said softly, "I can't do that. What would happen to my daughter? Who'd take care of her?"

"So . . . she's got a boyfriend, Mario. It happens . . . she's been alone a long time . . . it's not terrible, pal. But, there's somethin' else . . . he's black."

"A damn nig?"

"Don't say that, Mario. He's educated---a math teacher in the girls' school and a coach, too. I'm tellin' you what I know . . . what I looked into. The kids like him; he helps them when they're failin' with their schoolwork. He's been helpin' Christy and Georgiana. I never was much for school, and Rosie didn't stay in it long enough to be any help to Georgiana. I ain't heard anythin' bad about this guy. . . so calm down, Mario."

"Are you nuts, Augie? My wife's become a cryin' loony; she's fuckin' a black dude and you're askin' me to calm down? It's bad enough I have to watch my back, makin' sure I'm not spotted, do the dirty work for Richie Di. But now I gotta go back to Florida and find out what's happenin'."

"You don't have to, Mario. I'm keepin' an eye on things. I've been doin' it for awhile now—and that's only because it's for you—and it's your family."

Mario filled his glass again, held up the bottle to Augie, and at his nod, gave him another shot. "It would happen now. I just set up this woman—a seventy-year old, rich widow. I met her at a blackjack table in one of the casinos. I don't even remember which one; I was high. But she went for me like she was a teenager and I was the star of the football team. Even at her age, she's still attractive—kept her figure—dresses terrific. She's got homes in California and New York. Her husband was a movie agent, and it looks like he represented the right crowd. He left enough for her . . . and for me. I gotta work fast because she's here with some friends for only a few weeks."

"Sounds good. Too bad you think I spoiled it for you, my friend, but I'm sure you'd do the same for me—otherwise I wouldn' be here."

"Sure I would, Augie. As to this old bitch, I told her I was in real estate and just havin' some cash-flow problems this month. It's possible that I could have business in Florida. She might buy it. Ah, what the hell. If she's still here when I get back, that's terrific. If not, I'll find another broad with money. They're all over the place, and they're lonely, and they want sex. And I can give them that . . . and good, too."

The men looked at each other with knowing smiles, and Mario went on. "These women—they pick up the tabs, and they don't ask too many questions. I know I gotta dress well, and I do. I even rented a new Lexus so I look like I'm doin' great on my own."

"I noticed that Lexus parked between those pick-up trucks. I should have known it was yours, Mario. You ought to keep an eye on it with all those red necks around."

"What do I care? They steal it . . . that's the rental company's problem. I'll get another one." They both looked at each other and laughed and the tension broke. "Listen, Augie, I gotta thank you for carin' enough about me to come here and tell me all this."

"It's okay."

"I just gotta fly out as soon as I can and see what the story is for myself."

"What about you bein' wanted?"

"I think they're gonna give up lookin' for me soon, or they already have. There's bigger fish than me to catch. What I took from those thievin' bastards, they make back in a day. Besides, I got all kinds of new I.D. I paid for the best. I'll probably bleach my hair blonde again. I did it before—when I came here. I'll get some glasses and an attaché case, and I'll be a different person. The airports are lookin' for terrorists now. They're not hot for a guy involved in a car dealership heist. And those assholes are the ones they should be lookin' for. Blowin' up people all over our country is all those fucks can think of. There were plenty of them livin' in South Florida on 9/11, and I bet they got more there now."

"I don' doubt it," Augie said.

"There's stuff I have to take care of before I take off. I gotta see what jobs Richie Di has for me; maybe some knees will have to wait to be broken." They exchanged sly looks and were silent for a moment. "You know, Augie, Richie Di was the only one here who offered me work, and for that I gotta respect him."

"He'll understand if you wanna' tell him. Richie Di's got feelings for family. And you know, Mario, I'd like to put you up when you get to Florida, but it's just too risky. Our daughters come back to my house from school lotsa times and then we gotta deal with Rosie, too."

Mario said, "I know that Augie, holding up the bottle and asking for the third time, "Wan' another?"

"Nah, had enough, pal. Gotta return the car to Avis."

"I'd love to see Christy, and maybe I'll take that chance. But first, I'll rent a car and find a cheap motel. I'll be in for a few days. Won't take long for me to figure out what's goin' on. Like I said, if I lose this lady here, there's plenty more; I'll find another. She wasn' the first. I'm not gonna worry about it, Augie. But I made up my mind: Vegas is the place for me."

"Looks like you're on the right track this time, Mario. You finally hit what you can do best."

"I've got somethin' in mind regarding these women. I'm lookin' to score big and have nothin' more to do but live the good life. But I'll have to figure out those plans when I get back."

Augie stood up, Mario followed and hugs were exchanged. "I know—no phone calls, but you know where you can reach me. If you need me, Mario, leave word with Richie Di's place about where I can get you. I have to check in every day, anyway.'

Mario opened the door and a blast of hot air hit them. They both walked out; they passed some disheveled-looking men sitting on plastic chairs facing the empty pool. They glanced at Augie and Mario, and then returned to their conversation in low tones, passing around what looked like a fifth of gin. Mario and Augie, both in their early forties with physiques that shouted, 'don't fuck with me,' walked over to Augie's car.

"Thanks again, man," Mario said, as they shook hands.

"It's okay pal." Augie unlocked the door, started the engine and drove off.

ೞೲ   ೞೲ   ೞೲ

Pressing his foot down heavily on the gas pedal, Augie's head swam, one thought after another. I knew Mario would wanna come to Florida once he knew what was goin' on. This guy's a nut job and becomin' worse—he's done everything but kill, and now I wouldn' put that past him. What the hell is goin' on with his wife? She was smart and pretty—I coulda gone for her myself. Mario did a number on her, but wait a minute, he's my friend, not that screwed-up broad. Somehow, he felt that all this was going to lead to big trouble.

Augie was looking from side to side down the street as he was driving. He had to find a parking spot and call Agent Senewski, that FBI prick. Senewski had told him to phone his cell the minute he finished with Mario. He pulled over a few blocks later behind a dumpster and punched in Senewski's number. The connection was picked up immediately. "Senewski, it's me, Augie."

"Talk."

"Just left our friend. He's flyin' out like you wanted him to—in the next few days. He's makin' plans now. So, you can pick him up when he lands. I'm sure you got enough on him."

"Okay, Augie, we'll handle it from here. You're off the hook now for not reporting to your parole officer and a couple of other things I'm not even mentioning. But remember, we can have you taken in anytime for that violation which is serious enough to send you back."

"I gotcha."

"Just let me know when he contacts you in Florida. It's important."

"Sure, no problem, Senewski." Then he heard the click.

Augie put his cell in his shirt pocket and screamed, "That fuckin' son-of-a-bitch! He'll never let me go!"

Heading towards the Las Vegas Airport, he thought about the Witness Protection Program again. It might be what I'll have to do; Senewski mentioned it. If Mario or Richie Di finds out what I'm up to, I'll be a dead man. But, Rosie wouldn' ever agree to leave that nutty family of hers in Florida and Georgiana, leave her friends? Never! And even if I convinced them, they'd make my life a livin' hell. "FUCK!" Augie shouted, and banged the wheel with his fist as he pulled up to the RETURN gate for Avis.

12

Boca Raton, Florida

Yasin gently brushed a strand of Laila's silky, black hair from her face as she lay in a deep sleep beside him. She is so beautiful, he thought. And then his mind focused on the day's coming events, and he knew he could no longer sleep. Today they all were to meet with Nuri at his salon. He, Khaled, Harith Jacob, the architect, and Mansur Haskim, the construction foreman, were to be there. Mansur's true skill was with explosives, but today he would have to prove he was equally talented as an actor.

Harith, one of Iraq's most esteemed architects, was brought over from Iraq after Yasin chose him to be the one architect he wanted on his staff. Having him here gave their plan legitimacy. The fact that Harith did not willingly join them and would not see his family again until this job was completed didn't bother Yasin. His family was well provided for by the corporation, and with the situation as it now existed in Iraq, Harith should feel lucky that he and his loved ones were protected and still alive. The only concession Yasin made was allowing Harith limited phone conversations with his wife when he saw that depression was seriously affecting him. Yasin turned his back on the sleeping Laila and debated whether to bring her as well. They had to entrap Nuri. Laila had to come too. That was how it must be.

"Wake up, my darling," Yasin said quietly as he plied her face with soft kisses. We must get ready to see our friend. And we also have to pick up our famous architect."

Laila opened her eyes and asked, huskily, "Do I have to go?"

"Yes, my sweet. And you must look your most alluring self. Nuri must feel he would give up everything he has to possess you. You must seduce him with looks. He will be staring at your body and watching how you respond to him."

Laila rose slowly from the bed, her beige, silk gown clinging to her body and replied in a voice that could hardly be heard, "I'll do anything you want, Yasin; you know that."

Yasin looked at her and said nothing, but in his mind thoughts flashed like thunder bolts: Do not feel guilty now, after all these years. You rescued her from being nothing but a high-priced prostitute. After all you have given her, why stop using Laila for your purposes now? Even had she been able to leave what she was doing, the alternative would have been a life spent wearing a veil, married to a man who would beat her for whatever reason, whenever it suited him. She would have been made to grovel to get the simplest things.

Look what she possesses now, along with the fine education provided for her. When Laila first met people, they thought she was American; they could not detect even the slightest Middle Eastern accent. She'd also picked up the slang words and style of their language. Having done a good job convincing himself, Yasin dismissed his doubts and headed for the kitchen to make a fresh pot of coffee.

೮ಌ   ೮ಌ   ೮ಌ

A few hours later, two Mercedes drove to the Adam & Eve Beauty Salon and parked in the shopping center lot. Out of one car stepped Yasin, Laila and Harith. Out of the other, came Khaled and the burly Mansur. The architect carried his attaché with all he needed to make quick sketches. Mansur carried nothing, but his eyes took in everything. Walking briskly, they headed for the salon.

Nuri opened the door for them, a big smile on his face. "Come right in," he said. The five entered, each with a confident air . . . except for Laila, who looked sad, but stunning in tight jeans, high-heeled pumps and a white, sleeveless polo that called attention to her breasts. The men were dressed casually in slacks and sport shirts. After polite introductions to the two unknown to Nuri and handshakes all around, Nuri said, "First, let me show you my salon. Afterward we can see the vacant place next door; I have the key."

The salon was relatively small: reception area and desk, two stations for the stylists, manicure table, shampoo sinks, a combination storage/lunch room and a toilet. It seemed obvious to the group that Nuri's joyous attitude was because of possible backing that would enable him to add space, plus a whole new image for his salon.

The aromas of coconut, aloe and lillies prevailed throughout the shop. This was eliminated when they entered the premises that once had been the dry cleaning establishment. Chemical fumes lingered and piles of plastic coverings were strewn about. It looked like the previous tenants had left hurriedly. And so it was, as they all knew, except Nuri.

Everyone continued following Nuri as he walked and talked. He seemed overwhelmed by the very size of the place that could become his. Yasin noticed that when possible, Nuri's glance would go towards Laila, and then he'd fumble for the words he needed. That was good, he thought. Yasin observed Khaled watching everything closely, too.

The architect had a small pad in his hand and was busy making some drawings. The supposed construction manager was looking about and walking into every area Nuri excitedly showed him. Yasin, Laila and Khaled followed them. Taking Laila's hand in his, Yasin squeezed it gently. She looked up at him and smiled in return. Laila then called out, "Nuri, I'd like to hear what you have in mind. But maybe you need some input from a woman? After all, they make up most of your clientele."

Nuri stopped in his tracks and looked back at Laila. "You are right! Laila, please come over here. What do you think about luxurious, individual rooms for facials and massages in this area? I would like to pipe in sounds of waves rushing up on the shore. That is relaxing, is it not?"

"That's great, Nuri," Laila said. "Most women will love it, along with soft music, perhaps strings in the background."

"Sounds wonderful to me," Nuri replied. But, all the plans he had about the new salon and the remodeling left his mind. There was only one thought: He must have this woman. How could he do it? The thought plagued him. Just then, Laila appeared to have slipped on a wire hanger left on the floor.

Nuri helped her up at once and asked, "Are you okay, Laila?"

"I'm fine." She blushed, brushed herself off and said, "Thanks. Just felt a little queasy for a moment. And that hanger didn't help either."

He felt that she looked at him with kindness and interest. Could it be that she, too, had feelings for him? This was all too crazy, he thought. He had to focus on what was going on now. This was his chance of a lifetime . . . he just could not lose it. He turned to the architect, who continued to make notes. "Do you have enough there to go on?"

"Yes, Nuri, I believe so," Harith said, hesitantly, looking away from him.

Mansur was touching the walls, looking at the existing pipes, the air-conditioning ducts and said to no one in particular, "Looks good to me."

Yasin leaned against a wall filled with empty metal racks suspended from the ceiling and said quite loudly, "Nuri, I feel what you have in mind to do with this place will work—it will succeed! It really will be something."

Yasin needed a place that was undergoing construction as a front to give a group of men reason to gather and appear to be working. They actually would be furthering their own plans by preparing and familiarizing the men with all the materials needed for their offensive. Nuri Mustafa was a requirement for the overall plan. The construction of the new Adam & Eve Salon and Day Spa would fit in perfectly. And the people working at the salon, without exception, were now accomplices to murder and destruction.

13

Boca Raton, Florida

A few days later Yasin looked out the window towards the sea and the constant breaking waves on the shore. He wished his life ran as smoothly. He noticed that Khaled, sitting opposite him at the dining room table, had a pained expression on his face. Architectural plans relating to the salon lay spread out before them.

"Harith really worked this up well, did he not, Khaled?" Yasin asked as he glanced at the drawings.

Khaled nodded.

"I am going to call Nuri today. I told him we would have the plans, perhaps, before the end of the week. I will ask him to come over Thursday night after work. But first, I will phone Omar Youssef, our talented photographer, and make sure he is available for that night—although he knows better than to refuse me," Yasin added.

"Did you tell Laila yet?"

"She knows she has to do this. She has done it before. I stressed the fact to her that it is gravely important to have Nuri locked into us. And this film will do it," Yasin said, almost to himself.

He then looked directly at Khaled. "It is time for you to show your presence at the shop."

"Whenever you say."

"I am also phoning Nuri's three employees today, advising them that they will see you within the week, and again, to keep their mouths shut. They will be informed that you are a direct link to me. You will be introduced as the assistant to the architect. They will also be told that they are now under your observation and to await their orders. As customary, we will use them to purchase airline tickets, make hotel reservations, and buy anything we need—anything that might cause suspicion if done by a Middle Easterner. At this point, I am convinced they are frightened enough to do whatever we ask of them. This method has always worked, and it must work now."

"I agree," Khaled said, "And once we have the film, Nuri will be just as weak and ready to listen to our commands."

"I think we are finished for today," Yasin said. "Head home—go take a swim. You need a little time for yourself. I will be giving Laila the news, and we are better off alone. During the filming, of course, I will be at your apartment. I will tell Nuri an urgent business matter came up in New York and that I had to fly out Thursday morning for a day or two. I will tell him that Laila will explain everything, and that he can sign the papers so we can get started at once. I will also assure him that a lawyer is not necessary since they are simple agreements. Nuri will go along with that; he wants to enlarge his business more than anything. But not more than having Laila," Yasin added.

"Before I leave, Yasin, I must say this—I have concerns about Laila. I have never had this feeling before, and I know what she means to you. But her part is so important . . . what if she breaks down?"

"Khaled, it will not happen. I will talk to her and encourage her as I usually do. She will help us as she always has. I appreciate your telling me this, but do not worry."

"I apologize if I have gone too far."

"No need to apologize. This undertaking is our biggest yet, and I can always sense if something is going wrong. If I do suspect that she is having problems, I will resolve them."

They grasped each other's shoulders as they often did when parting—only this time, when Yasin turned away, his eyes held tears.

Khaled walked to the door. At the sound of it closing, a rather sad voice came from the balcony. "Yasin, are you through? I have to speak with you."

"Certainly, my darling. Khaled just left."

He walked briskly to the balcony. Laila was stretched out on a cushioned chaise, wearing a black, strapless sundress and red sandals. In her lap was a new French novel and in her hand, a glass of lemonade.

"What is it, Laila? You sound unhappy," Yasin asked, as he lay down on the matching chaise next to hers.

She placed the book and the glass on a small table beside her and looked directly at him. Tears welled up in her eyes. "You know why. It's the photo shoot that's being planned. I can't go through with it."

"Why? You have done this many times before. It is a one-hour acting job at the most. There is nothing to feel ashamed about."

"Yasin, my love, you have to understand. I must be honest with you. I know I've done these things before at your request. I was uncomfortable, but I did them."

"You have to now, as well, my dear. Nuri is an absolute necessity to this job of ours. He must be terrified enough to submit to what is asked of him and to never give up any information. The filming of the lovemaking is what will do it. It always does."

"I just can't," Laila said quietly and turned her face away from him.

"My darling, you know how complex this plan is. Arrangements have already been made for our so-called workers to report to the construction site once Khaled is in place. Some are here in Florida. More will be flying in. All will be trained well for what they have to do, even though they will look and act like ordinary laborers. We have paid out large amounts of money to secure the building permits. You know what it will look like—like it is really going to happen."

"Can't we find another place, another person? He's just too innocent. I can't do it to him."

"That is impossible! Are you crazy? To work Nuri into this plan was a demand that I accepted. It is a demand I cannot change. I gave my word. Furthermore, he is not as innocent as you think. I choose not to tell you all of this for your own good. But believe me, he will be getting what he deserves."

Silence took a seat between them. Yasin broke it with, "It is only a short period of time out of your day, my princess. You know how much I need you and how I love you. I am sorry, but now I cannot discuss this any longer. I must make some calls. Relax for awhile," he added, putting his hand on her neck and massaging it gently after feeling the tightness. He then turned her face to his, knelt down and kissed her lips softly. As Yasin stepped away, he forced himself to smile at Laila. He noticed she picked up the iced glass of lemonade, pressed it against her forehead and looked back at him expressionless. Inwardly, he was seething.

He walked into his office, sat down behind his desk, and removed a bottle of Johnny Walker from his bottom drawer. He put the bottle to his mouth and swallowed. As the heat of the drink took control of his body, he calmed down, accepting that this was not going to be easy. What bothered him more was how he had let the situation develop into what it was now. He knew he'd seen it coming, and, done nothing about it. Perhaps it was too late, he thought.

He phoned Khaled on his cell. "You were right. There is a crisis here. We may have to delay awhile."

"Whatever you think best, Yasin. You have always done it right."

"Well, Khaled, my record of successes is being challenged now. I must think. I will get back to you in a few hours."

Yasin hung up, took his gold letter opener in his right hand, and jammed the point into his ring finger—hard enough to draw blood. I cannot let this woman stop me, he thought, as he sucked the blood from his fingertip. I will reach her yet, and if not? And if not . . .? And with that thought, he laid his head on his desk, restraining the urge to hurt himself badly.

14

Several miles from Yasin and Laila's plush condo in Boca Raton was the Linton Boulevard Medical Complex in Delray Beach. Suite 207 in the 7258 Building was like any other office in the complex, except the door read, Pro Healthcare Services. Behind all the other doors were the usual medical doctors: urologists, internists, dermatologists, and ophthalmologists—alone or in a group. Suite 207 was one of the few offices listed on the main floor directory that did not actually house a physician. It was a Homeland Security off-site location.

Agent Kevin Walsh, a former Army Captain, sat at his desk in one of the small rooms that made up the suite. He was short, but wiry; his red hair was buzz-cut. A rather exotic-looking man sat across from him. He was in his late twenties, muscular, and covered with tattoos. His coloring was dark, and his right foot was in constant motion. Born to a Cuban mother and a Syrian father, his name was Carlos Hamed.

A few minutes before, Carlos had frightened a group of elderly men and women when he dashed up the two flights of steps. Most, near the staircase, were either sitting in wheel chairs accompanied by Jamaican or Haitian aides behind them, or holding onto walkers as they waited for the elevator.

"So, Carlos, you're in my office now, like you wanted. What's that important?"

"You know, man, I'd never come here if I could have told you this on the phone."

"I'm listening. Go ahead."

"I was in a bar last night in Belle Glade that gets a lot of South American illegals. Hung out there for about forty minutes—had a beer—didn't notice anything unusual, so I figured I'd leave for a dive in Riviera Beach. Nothin' goin' on there either, so I didn't even finish that beer. Decided to make one last stop at a Delray Beach joint where there's a mix of guys. Ordered my third beer of the night, and this one I planned on finishing." Carlos smiled at the Agent, but no smile was returned.

"Cut the shit. Just tell me what has you so riled up."

"Listen, man, don't get upset—I got to tell you how this happened. I was sitting at the bar and watching the door when three drunken dudes stumble in. They don't fit in with the construction or landscape workers who hang out there. They looked Middle Eastern, and their hands were too clean to have done much manual labor."

Agent Walsh perked up at this last piece of information.

"Only one of them spoke English, and not good. The two others, I know, were speaking Arabic. I hung on their every word. It was hard to make out because I wasn't close enough to them."

"So, what the fuck is it, already?" the Agent asked.

"Okay, take it easy. They were getting mad because Jimmy, the bartender, wasn't too happy about serving them drinks. And he wanted the money up front before they got their beers. That really pissed them off." Carlos paused for a few seconds and then asked Walsh, "Got a cigarette? I just ran out."

Walsh took the half-empty pack of Kent's on his desk and shoved it over to Carlos, who pulled one out, lit it with his Ronson, took a deep drag and went on. "Anyway, man, after the guys finally got their beers, one of them started yelling in Arabic at the bartender. His friend told him to shut up. But he didn't. Now I heard every word 'cause most of the fellas, who were hanging around the bar area, had gone. Screaming in Arabic, he said something like, 'Once we blow up your bridges, you pigs, we will have you on your knees, and I will have enough money to buy this shithole, if I want to. Fuck you all!'

"Then the guy who spoke a little English looked like he was ready to hit this loudmouth. But instead, he told them very strongly that they had to get out of there now, and they did. I left some money on the bar and walked out too, but not fast 'cause everybody left was just staring at each other. Look, I'm sure I was the only one there who understood them, so no one knew what this guy said. So that's why I'm here. I got the tag number and make of their truck," Carlos took a slip of paper from his shirt pocket and handed it to Walsh.

"Okay, you did a good job, and you'll be well paid for your work, as you always are." Walsh sounded calm, but his face paled and his hands trembled slightly. "Remember, Carlos, whatever you say here is never to be repeated."

"Sure, Boss, and you don't have to tell me that every time." Serious looks were exchanged.

Another one of his informants had referred Carlos Hamed to Walsh. The man knew he wanted someone who understood and spoke Arabic. Carlos came with a bonus because not only did he understand and speak Arabic, but Spanish too. Since he had only occasional jobs house painting, Carlos was happy about the extra bucks he was making by finding information to give Walsh. He received orders, but sometimes he picked up something on his own.

"You can go now, Carlos . . . and, thanks." He offered his hand, which was shaken firmly. "You'll hear from me when I have the cash for you."

"See you, man." He got up, walked to the door, unlocked it with familiarity and made his way out.

Kevin Walsh was single, forty-two and had been a career man in an Intelligence Unit of the United States Army. He reached the rank of Captain and served his country in many hotbed places. The last was Afghanistan. His ability was well known to his superiors during the time he spent with Intelligence. Regardless, after his twenty years were up, he wanted to leave the military; he'd had it. Kevin was anxious to lose some of the bad memories that haunted him. He welcomed civilian life and thought perhaps he'd open a business—what kind? He didn't know. But a personal tragedy ended all his aspirations.

After his separation from active service, he was approached by an Agent of Homeland Security to head a rather obscure office in Delray Beach, Florida. They knew all about his family and particularly about his sister, Kathryn. It was unlikely that he'd refuse to work for them, and they were right. He was now in a Joint Terrorism Task Force Unit that was involved in finding and investigating illegal aliens with any possible connections to terrorist groups.

ഇൻൻ   ഇൻൻ   ഇൻൻ

Kevin Walsh came from a large Irish-American family. He had four brothers and two sisters. Kathryn, unmarried, the youngest at twenty-five, was a stockbroker who'd been unemployed for some time due to her company's downsizing. After a fourth interview, Cantor Fitzgerald had hired her. It was a prestigious New York City bond-trading firm located on the top floors of Building One in the World Trade Center.

Kathryn's blue eyes gleamed with excitement when she told the family at Sunday dinner, "I've got it! I'm hired!" Her bright red hair and good figure always brought Kathryn stares. All her brothers were protective, but Kevin, the most.

"When will you be starting, Kath?" Kevin asked. He was on leave and glad to be home.

"Next Monday, a week from tomorrow," she said, smiling, looking around the table.

September 10th, 2001, was Kathryn Walsh's first day at Cantor Fitzgerald. Her second day, September 11th, was her last. Kathryn was one of those who'd jumped from the building to her death as the flames rose behind her.

15

North Miami Beach, Florida

Kevin Walsh burst through the door of Peter Senewski's FBI office in North Miami, making even the tough-looking, big guy Senewski jump. They had been working together for sometime now since the FBI and Homeland Security shared information on particular task force assignments.

"Sit down, Kevin, relax a moment. You sounded like you really had a lead when you phoned. I left word to let you in the minute you got here, but I didn't think you'd make it from Delray this fast."

Kevin sat in the chair opposite Peter, but looked like he was going to pop up momentarily. "Peter, I have this gut feeling that we're onto something. Let me explain. One of my informants was at a bar in Delray Beach. Three guys came in towards the end of the evening, looking like they already had too much to drink and started shooting off their mouths to the bartender." Kevin went on with the entire story Carlos had told him. He said that his source reported the men were Middle Eastern and, except for one, spoke little English.

"Look, we can't jump on guys because they're drunk and come from an Arab country."

"It's not that, Pete. My informant understands and speaks Arabic and Spanish, but he looks like some South American illegal. He heard everything one guy screamed before another spoke to him in Arabic, told him to shut up, and they all left. I told you the whole conversation, and I've also got it recorded—even brought it with me. Want to hear it?"

"Not necessary, Kevin. Just leave the recording with me, and if I have to prove your point, it might help."

"Fine, take it." Kevin opened his attaché, pulled out the recording and handed it over to Peter. And then without pausing, Kevin added, "And what makes it worse is that these aren't ignorant young boys who were promised seventy-two virgins when they become martyrs. These guys are obviously paid killers. They're not looking to die—they're looking to make a bundle from blowing up bridges—if this is true. They may not speak English well, but they were probably trained in Pakistan and adept at planting explosives."

"Okay, Pete, calm down a minute. Do you have anything else?"

"Sure do. When one of the guys told the other two in Arabic that they must get out of the bar at once, my man was on them. He paid his bill and left. They were walking and arguing and he had the time to get the tag number and the description of their truck. My office traced the plate and the truck is registered to a construction company. It's currently used for work at this crummy, little beauty parlor in Delray called Adam & Eve. I went over there and they've got legit permits hanging on the next-door property. The sign in the window says that it's to be enlarged to a luxury salon and day spa.

If Kevin hadn't been so excited, he might have noticed Peter's face lose its color. This was surprising since he was trained to be aware of these things. Only a few seconds passed. Peter composed himself, looked straight at Kevin and said, "So? So far, it seems innocent. Companies get construction workers from all over the world. I've seen Russian, Ukrainian, Polish, Spanish and even a few Americans."

He smiled at Kevin then, but Kevin didn't respond—just looked at his notes seriously. Peter spoke after a few seconds.

"These guys were drunk, you were saying? Maybe they were trying to throw a scare into the bartender or the people around."

"Not when they're speaking Arabic and think they're safe because no one understands them, and there's more, Peter. The owner of the beauty parlor is from Iraq. I want to know if there's something going on there beside the expansion."

"Listen, Kev, I know you get stirred up when you think you've got something hot, but have a little patience. Let me see what I can find out. It may be something and then you're right. But it may be nothing, as usual. Leave whatever else you have with me, and I'll get right on it."

Kevin Walsh pulled some additional papers from his attaché—placed them on the agent's desk, got up and walked towards the door. As it was closing, he turned around and said, "Let me hear from you as soon as you learn anything."

"Of course, Kev. Will do."

Peter read the papers Kevin left behind and then added the recording to the pile. He'd heard right. Listed was Adam & Eve, the beauty salon where he'd found Mario Giamonte's wife, Theresa, working. He'd questioned her at the shop when Mario's caper was still under investigation. That young Arab owner had been there as well. He remembered him.

After slamming his fist on the desk, he picked up the same cell phone he used when Augie Costellano called the week before. That was when Augie told him he'd been successful in getting Mario set on returning to Florida. Usually Peter held onto a cell phone for only a short period of time, then destroyed it and replaced it with a new one. But he'd kept this one longer because it was the only number Augie could use to contact him. He took the cell in his hands, which were now sweaty, and punched in the numbers. After a few rings, the call was answered.

"Yasin, it's Peter."

"If you are calling, it looks like a nice day to meet on the beach," he said, in a strong voice that didn't match the carefree words.

"Right, Yasin. Same place—around five o'clock—okay?"

"See you there, my friend."

16

Boca Raton, Florida

Laila seemed to drift into Yasin's office retreat, looking sluggish. Her hair was messy, her satin robe was creased, and she was barefoot, instead of wearing her customary, high-heeled, satin mules. She sat down on the chair across from him.

Yasin had just hung up after speaking to Peter Senewski. He, too, looked strange—unhappy and puzzled. "Laila, are you getting dressed? It is late afternoon, but you have been going around like this for the past two days. What is bothering you, my darling?"

"I've been depressed over several things, but thought them through, and I'm here to apologize to you for my actions."

"What did this to you?"

"The planned event with Nuri brought on this depression, and I felt I couldn't do it." Yasin sat there, staring at her, saying nothing. Laila knew that by this admission, she was leaving herself open for his forgiveness or his rage. But she was also aware that she couldn't go on if she kept it all inside. She was ready to crack.

"Why, Laila? You have handled these situations before with little problem. You know how important it is for me to gain complete control of Nuri—and this is the only way."

"I understand that. But for some reason, my mind kept drifting back to Iraq before evil entered my life—before you

84

saved and protected me. Laila propped her legs under her on the seat, looked directly at Yasin, and continued.

"I remembered my home, my parents, my sisters and brothers. I recalled going to school—the boys in one building and the girls in the other. Then there were the hot summer nights when the family put our beds on the open rooftop, and it was such fun to sleep there. That was the time when my father was working as a baker, before the owner replaced him with his son. You know he never worked again."

"I thought about the wonderful meals my mother made," Laila continued, "I could almost smell the aroma of her lamb, rice and spinach dish that was my favorite. Her baklava was the best I ever tasted. The neighbors were always welcome to visit; tea and cakes were always served. My father had done well in that bakery, plus there were all those sweets he brought home for us. We were all so happy then."

"Laila, what has this all to do with what is happening now? How does this affect the job we must do and the task you have been given?"

"My dear Yasin—I'm through thinking back. I came to the realization that those memories are all behind me. I can treasure them, but you're the only one I love in all the world. You saved my life, and for that I'll always be grateful. You've given me more that I ever imagined—teachers, who have imparted their wisdom to me plus anything I ever ask for. I've always had your love and devotion. I can only repay you by doing whatever you ask without question, and I'm now ready."

Yasin let out a deep sigh, stood up from behind his desk and took Laila in his arms. "Darling girl of mine, you are forgiven," he whispered in her ear.

"I'm so glad I told you all that was in my heart. I feel so much better," she said, wiping tears from her eyes with her hand.

He held her closer and kissed her open lips. Laila responded warmly.

What Laila didn't mention to Yasin was that the most troubling aspect of what she was asked to do was Nuri. This man she had to make love to, the man with whom she felt such a kinship, was also a man who physically attracted her. That had never happened since she met Yasin. This was what she'd have to resolve herself. The "how" was the question she still pondered as Yasin picked her up and carried her into their bedroom.

ೞ೦೧ ೞ೦೧ ೞ೦೧

Soon after their lovemaking, Yasin left Laila in a peaceful sleep. He showered and dressed in a sweat suit. Returning to his desk, he picked up his cell phone and placed a call.. "Khaled—you'll have to join me about five tonight, on the beach in Delray, the same place we go when we meet our special friend."

"Problem, Yasin?"

"Looks like it. I know nothing more as yet. Remember to dress for walking on the beach. This may take some time."

"I will see you there."

Yasin snapped the phone shut and sat there looking perturbed. He was glad Laila was out of her black mood. Entirely? He wasn't convinced. But Peter getting in touch with him meant trouble, and that he didn't like. He opened his deep, desk drawer, removed the bottle of Dewers and took a long swig. A feeling of euphoria overcame him. He knew it would remain only a short time, but he relished every moment.

17

North Miami Beach, Florida

As Yasin was enjoying the warmth of his Scotch, Peter Senewski was wishing he had a bottle stashed in his office. But the FBI frowned upon their agents consuming alcohol during work hours, and Peter adhered to that rule though quite a few of the men didn't. It was only when Peter was completely shaken that he needed a drink. He opened the folder on Kevin Walsh that he'd just retrieved from the files. As he turned page after page, reading each one thoroughly, Peter found nothing to use to discredit him. Perhaps Kevin's overzealousness might be the key. He knew he would have to find something if what Kevin had discovered was true.

"Shit!" Peter said aloud as he slammed the dossier closed. Why the hell did he have to bring this poor bastard down? Kevin was strung out from his sister's death on 9/11 and was basically a good guy, and Peter was trying to frame him. This is what Yasin has finally done to me, he thought.

He started sweating heavily as his mind went back eight years to the time when he'd been working as a Director of Security for several American firms doing business in Cairo. Peter was a former Navy Seal, who had seen action in Desert Storm. He was tough and knowledgeable. His job then was to set up a strong security staff for whatever company employed him and then move on to the next firm that needed his expertise. In his position he met many wealthy Middle Eastern businessmen, and one of them was Yasin Adeeb. After working all day with some of the security people at one of Yasin's plants, who should walk in as the last meeting ended, but Yasin himself, greeting him cordially.

"Come to my apartment this evening, Peter. I am having a few friends over; please join us all for dinner as my guest. Most of the men are big in manufacturing or exporting, and they probably could use your services. It is a good way to meet them and to promote your company and yourself."

"That's very kind of you, Yasin," Peter said. They'd known each other for some time by then, and they were on a first-name basis.

"It is my pleasure. I like you, Peter. You are doing a good job for me, and I would like to get more business contacts for you." Yasin then pulled a white card from his breast pocket and handed it to Peter. On it was Yasin's name, home address and phone number. "Come around seven."

If only he'd slipped and broken his leg that evening before he left for Yasin's apartment, he thought, how different his life would be now. Peter recalled the events of that night vividly. He'd taken a cab to Yasin's luxury residence and had been impressed immediately. Upon entering the plush apartment, Peter observed the thick Persian rugs, finely-made furniture, lavish draperies. Yasin appeared delighted to see him, introduced him to the three other men there, along with two beautiful, obviously Arab, young women dressed in what looked like the latest Paris fashions. They were not the usual party girls.

The men continued their conversations, and Yasin offered Peter a drink. For a moment he'd forgotten how strange it was to see Muslim men drinking like this and flirting with these beauties. But who was he to judge, he thought. He noticed the men acted like they'd already had too much. "Thanks, Yasin. Scotch on the rocks, if you have it," he said.

"If I have it? I have it all, Peter."

Yasin poured Peter's drink, handed it to him and said, "Cheers!" as you Americans say or is it the British?"

"We both do—makes no difference. "Cheers!" Peter said with feeling and tapped Yasin's glass with his. This may be a really great night, he'd thought. With Yasin pitching for me, things will fall into place.

"Have some appetizers, Peter." He noticed a silver tray full of pita triangles, olives, hummus and stuffed peppers on the coffee table, along with small plates, forks and napkins.

The men continued with their drinking, smoking and talking. Little attention was paid to Peter, although Yasin introduced him warmly. He felt excluded, he remembered, and Yasin, noticing Peter's discomfort, went back to speak with him. "All the people here have an understanding of English and speak it, but there are some who do better than others," Yasin explained. "They will try conversing with you as the evening goes on; you will see."

At that moment, one of the men slapped the woman he was talking to so hard that she fell to the floor, her cheek swelling and blood oozing from her mouth. In a second, Peter was at the woman's side, helping her up and giving her the handkerchief from his back pocket. She took it, nodded her thanks and appeared groggy.

"Get her some ice!" Peter yelled out as he helped the young woman to a chair. Then he approached the man who'd hit her. The man had his back turned to him. Without hesitation, Peter recalled the moment he'd pulled him around so they faced each other. "What the hell did you think you were doing? Where I come from you don't slap women around. You have respect for them."

"Who are you to tell me what to do? You, American pig! You infidel! She did not want me to fuck her, the bitch. What else is she here for then?" Looking directly at Peter, he added, "Take your hand off me now, or I will kill you!"

Yasin had walked over to the two, saying, "Najid, calm down. You know when you have had too much liquor you lose your temper. Peter, just relax. I will take care of this."

That was about all the time Yasin had to speak, Peter remembered, because Najid pulled out a switchblade from his pants' pocket and pressed the button, opening it instantly. He lashed out at Peter, but the heavy alcohol consumption obviously ruined his aim. He only managed to graze Peter's shoulder. Within seconds Peter had twisted Najid's wrist until it cracked. Najid cried out in pain and dropped the knife. Peter knew now that he should have stopped there. But he hadn't. He constantly replayed the next thing he did: He'd thrown Najid to the floor with a strength and force he'd used only in desperate situations. Then he'd stomped his foot on Najid's neck and broke it.

Though he'd been introduced to him, he was unaware that Najid Abdulah was a wealthy rug exporter—a bachelor, known for his flagrant abuse of women, hard drinking and quick temper. Again, he thought, if he'd only known this then. The attempt on his life had overwhelmed him completely. He'd remained standing over the body in a state of shock.

The others, except for the bruised young woman, who was still seated, appeared frozen. Yasin knelt to take Najid's pulse, although it was a foregone conclusion that he was dead. He shook his head negatively. Yasin then stood up and spoke intensely and without hesitation in Arabic to the men and women. Peter believed he'd spoken in Arabic to make things perfectly clear. After Yasin's short talk, they took no further notice of Peter or the body. They simply nodded affirmatively to everything Yasin said and made their way to the front door. One of the men helped the injured young woman; he took her arm, and her friend assisted.

As the door closed behind them, Yasin shrugged and said, "Peter sit down. These things happen. Let me get you another Scotch. Najid was like a stick of dynamite waiting to be lit and explode. I knew he would go off sometime, but I did not think, tonight. And I did not know he carried a knife."

"Yasin, what troubles me now is if you knew Najid was so anti-American, why did you invite me when he was here? Did you think he'd possibly attempt to kill me, but I'd kill him instead? Was he someone you wanted to put away?"

There was no response from Yasin to the question. He simply grinned and shoved the glass into Peter's hand. He then poured another Scotch for himself. "For a man whose life I intend to protect from the authorities, you appear to be acting rather strangely."

Peter knew if the press got hold of this, the headlines in tomorrow's papers, both Arabic and English, would tell of an American murdering an Egyptian. Self-defense in Egypt was a touchy judicial issue of which he was aware. Receiving death threats and seeing his career demolished would probably be next.

Forcing himself to sit down and sip the fine Scotch, he said, "This isn't the first time someone's tried to kill me, Yasin. And more than one has wound up like Najid. As you saw, I can handle it, but I do thank you for stepping in and dealing with your friends. Whatever you told them, you seem to have put them in eternal fear. But I'm sorry to say from my training, this looks like a set-up."

"Take it easy, Peter," Yasin said. "It was not, and those who were here know full well to say nothing about this incident. They were told bluntly what their fate and that of their families would be if they did."

Yasin then excused himself, took his drink, went into another room, and Peter heard him on the phone. A few minutes later he returned and sat down on a chair facing Peter. "Everything will be taken care of, my friend. I have engaged the services of two men who will dispose of the body, and Najid Abdulah will no longer be a problem. They will be here shortly, and be assured—they are experts."

"I owe you, Yasin."

"Peter, it is okay. You owe me nothing. However, in the future if I need you, I expect you to be there for me."

"Of course," he'd responded, knowing that Yasin had now claimed his soul. Peter had wanted to get out of there immediately, but his eyes stayed riveted to the body, stiffening by the minute. A little blood had seeped through Peter's shirt from his minor shoulder wound. Yasin noticed it and said, "Let me attend to your injury."

"It's nothing. I'm leaving now anyway. I'll take care of it when I get home."

"Do as you wish, but do not worry so. This was self-defense. Do not feel bad for what has happened to this mad man." He continued, "In Cairo, people disappear all the time. Questions may be asked at first, but they will end shortly. The authorities will surmise that he was kidnapped, and they will wait to hear if there was a ransom demand sent to his company. When none appears, they will eventually close the case as an unexplained disappearance."

Soon after Yasin had spoken, the doorbell rang. Two young men in work clothes, one carrying a small, black, zippered bag were ushered in. They said little but went to their job immediately. Pushing the body into the middle of the rug, they removed every piece of furniture sitting on it. Then they rolled it up with the corpse securely inside. Taking a large, black plastic sheet and heavy rope from their zippered bag, they wrapped the plastic around the rug, tying it tightly with the rope in three places. Then they returned the furniture to its original position. Each man lifted an end of the rug and put it on his shoulder. One bent down to pick up the black bag, and they walked quickly out the front door.

That evening changed Peter's life completely. His greatest concern immediately afterward was for his love, Azhar Aalim, a translator who worked for Yasin. The man, himself, had introduced her to him. Peter couldn't believe he'd fallen so in love with this beautiful, Muslim woman. Educated in England, she was the oldest of five children. Coming from a middle-class family, she was grateful for her education and for the opportunity Yasin had given her. It was just a few weeks since Peter had met her, but he was convinced she was the only woman for him. Their romance had flourished—or as much as it could flourish in Egypt. He knew he had to speak to her that evening.

The next day he made plans to return to the United States. Peter was suave at handling people, and he arranged for his company to transfer him back home. Despite her family's disapproval, he convinced Azhar of his love and plans to marry her. Azhar left Cairo after he resolved all the paperwork and flew to him. Difficult as all of this was, he accomplished it in a record-breaking few months. Peter had called in every favor owed him, greased palms and pulled strings. They were married as soon as possible after Azhar set foot on U.S. soil. Now they were parents of a handsome, outgoing three-year old son, and they had another on the way.

Peter continued working as a Security Director; he had no problem in obtaining positions. Yasin kept in touch with him over the years, followed his progress, and was delighted when the FBI recruited Peter. His background was thoroughly investigated since it's rare for an agent to be married to a Muslim woman. He was found to be completely clean. In fact, Azhar was cleared also to act as an interpreter, when needed, because of her command of Arabic and her translation skills.

Upon entering the FBI four years earlier, Peter was forced to feed information to Yasin by strong, personal threats, and there seemed to be no end in sight. He was also made privy to some of Yasin's current plans, minimally, so he could alert him if he knew of any leak. True, the money he received bought them many things—a house with an ocean view in North

Miami, a boat and the BMW he was driving. But it never made up for his spying activities and the lying to Azhar. She was prying him with even more questions lately.

Just last night, she'd asked: "Peter, where are we getting this money to buy these luxuries? You know we really do not need them. I am so happy with you and Jameel. With a new baby coming, should we not we stop this wild spending?"

He'd taken her in his arms and said, "Don't worry; I'm working extra assignments that entitle me to bonuses. This is earned money, and there's nothing to be upset about, Azhar." His wife was intelligent and now suspicious. He could feel it. His words comforted her temporarily, but keeping his dark secret was getting more difficult.

Peter's gut feeling was that the information Kevin Walsh had would be a turning point in his life. Yasin had to be stopped now if he was involved in this new development. More important was the fact that he also had to get Azhar and his son out of the house, move them to another area, as far away as possible.

He hated himself for what he'd done and knew he couldn't go on like this any longer. Chills replaced the sweats he had. He felt the same as he had before a combat mission. He fought the feeling, but it overtook him. He knew he'd have to tell Azhar the truth. But for now, he'd think up a story about the move and that's all he'd tell her. Any further plans would take every bit of ingenuity he had, and he needed time.

Peter also knew what would happen if Yasin, along with every one of his men, weren't apprehended. Once he was found to be the one who turned them in, Peter would pay with his life and that of his wife and son, as well as Azhar's family in Cairo. Yasin had threatened him with this when he was originally approached.

The thought of anything happening to his family sent another chill through him. What Yasin had asked of him before was a demand with no choice. Now, the possible threat to thousands went beyond his family. This new revelation could possibly be the planning of another 9/11. And no matter what the danger was to his loved ones and himself, Peter was convinced he was the only one who could prevent it. But was that possible? If not, perhaps he'd have to develop another means for he and his family to escape the upcoming madness.

18

After the call to Khaled, Yasin continued going over his plans and checking to see that work on the salon was going according to their time schedule, though it seemed to him that the clock was not moving this afternoon. He knew Khaled was there daily, watching every detail. Yasin was feeling weary, though, of his responsibilities. The foundations and religious organizations that backed these ventures were extremely demanding. Yasin had to fully substantiate expenses, and the higher-ups' requirements constantly increased. They paid him astronomical amounts of money, but one failure and it might all end.

Every so often Yasin got up to check on Laila. She lay there like an Egyptian Queen, he thought, after his last glance in the bedroom. Only pills could bring on such a deep sleep, he told himself. This again was disturbing because he couldn't count on her being as stable as she insisted she was. Perhaps it was the upcoming meeting that was making him so unnerved.

He went into the kitchen and snacked on yogurt and chopped cucumbers, stopping to make a fresh pot of coffee.

Back at his desk, his mug beside him, he called Khaled. "I think we ought to go over a few things before we meet our friend. Come as soon as you can. Will that be a problem?"

"No, not at all. I will be there soon."

Yasin scrutinized the papers before him. A sudden rustling caused him to look up. There stood Laila in her workout clothes. "I'm going to my exercise class now. I really need it," she said cheerfully.

"Of course, my dear, that is fine. I will not be home for dinner though. Something came up that needs my attention. But, there is that Greek yogurt you like, salty olives and stuffed grape leaves to tempt you. I shopped a little early this morning."

"That was nice of you, my darling, but don't worry; I'll be okay. I'm trying to eat less and exercise more. And sometimes I don't even feel like eating." She then went over to his desk, carrying her gym bag, and kissed him long and hard.

"After that, my dear Laila, how do you expect me to let you go?"

"I'll be here when you get back," she replied and gave him the beautiful smile he adored.

"One thing, my darling—when you return please telephone Nuri and tell him to come over on Tuesday evening, when he is finished with work. Tell him he has to initial the final plans for the additional expansion. You know I will not be here, and you know what to tell him about my being called to Tampa on some important, unexpected business problem. Omar will get here in the late afternoon and will set up his photography equipment in our bedroom closet. The whole event should take less than an hour. You know the routine," Yasin said looking straight at her. "When you are sure about Nuri coming, please phone Omar."

Laila looked down. "Of course," she said, and after a few seconds went by, she swung her bag over her shoulder and walked out. Security phoned, announcing Khaled's arrival just as Laila left.

A few minutes later, Khaled, wearing a designer sweat suit, appeared at Yasin's door. Once inside he said, "I met Laila at the elevator, Yasin, and she looked a little distressed."

"She said she is fine, Khaled. Let us leave it at that . . . for now. Come, my boy, we have to discuss some things that are bothering me." One of those was the ominous feeling he had about the meeting, but Yasin was going to keep that to himself. Khaled nodded and followed him to his office.

ഇരുഷ   ഇരുഷ   ഇരുഷ

About 6:30 PM, the three men could be seen walking along the shore at Delray Beach. Across the street from them was Boston's, a restaurant where a younger crowd gathered in couples or with friends to sit, drink and take in the ocean air. Although the setting was beautiful, Peter, Yasin and Khaled did not look like a happy three-some. They appeared too serious.

Peter was walking, breathing hard and speaking not too quietly. "I've told you everything that Kevin Walsh told me, and I believe this guy. He's always suspicious, but this time I feel he's onto something real, and in progress. I just know it!" Though there were few people walking on the beach, Yasin gave Peter a look that toned down his next remark.

"I'm looking into the situation myself," Peter continued, "So there'll be no other agent on this. One good thing is that each FBI office doesn't know what another is doing. They're all separate units—functioning independently unless you ask another one to take action or cover leads for you. I have all the information—no one else does. The questioning I'll do is commonplace. We do it all the time on possible leads."

"From what you have told me, I think this may become a problem for us. However, the important thing is to stop it now," Yasin said, as he kicked away a large seashell with deadly force. Khaled, as usual, said nothing, but he caught Yasin's eye, and that confirmed that he too was aware of the danger in this situation.

"Is there anything you can find on this Kevin Walsh to discredit him?"

Peter looked down and said, "Yasin, unfortunately, this guy is spotless. I knew it, but I checked his records anyway. The only thing is that he has a personal vendetta. His sister was killed in one of the Towers on 9/11, and he's now out for blood."

"Perhaps, Peter, he can be made to look as if he is paranoid—sees terrorist cells starting where none exists—that he has done it before and so is not reliable."

"I'm considering every angle. I never ask you anything about your work, Yasin, but from the information I've just given you, could this mean another 9/11 is in the making?"

"What I do and how I work is not a matter of your concern. Your job is to supply me with facts that I need or request and I will take it from there. I told you I am here in Florida on business and recently undertook the building of a salon and spa in Delray, to replace the Adam and Eve Beauty Shop."

"Understood."

"Peter, you are a wealthy man, living in a magnificent home, owning a luxury car and boat. And on top of that you have a beautiful, intelligent wife and a wonderful son—with another child on the way. You have every comfort, and I have seen to that for the past several years. Frankly, I do not like it when attention is drawn to possible terrorist activities. It is not good for any enterprise, my friend," Yasin said as he gave Peter an affectionate pat on the back.

"I knew you'd be upset, but that you'd also want to know what I learned."

"You did right, Peter."

"When I get back to my office, I'll make some calls and, Yasin, I'll be in touch."

The three men stood at the water's edge and shook hands. Two headed one way and the third, another. As Yasin and Khaled walked towards the car parked in one of the metered spots on A1A, Yasin said, "If this job is called off because of the big mouth of one man, it will be our doom, Khaled. This plan is costing millions in training, supplies, set-ups like Nuri's salon, and heavy payoffs."

"We may be able to stop the investigation at this point, but more of a concern to me is Peter. Do you think he can still be trusted?" Khaled asked.

"Peter owes me his life and for that I own him. He would be in prison or dead if I had not acted quickly. We need him, and if he talks, he knows he will be removed along with his immediate family and that of his wife's." Almost to himself, he said, "That would be too bad—I have known her family for years." As the two men reached the car, Yasin opened the door and got behind the wheel. Khaled said, "If you will allow me, I would like to tell you of my feelings."

"Of course. We can sit here for awhile."

"I do not know how far we can push Peter. I feel he is thinking of turning. As you mentioned to him, it has been years that he has been a paid informant. This piece of information he gave us may be his last. Something in his manner betrayed him. As for that Kevin Walsh, from what Peter said, he is too volatile. He has personal reasons for his investigation. He will always be difficult as long as he is with Homeland Security."

"You are right, Khaled. I am giving this thought too. Peter was well compensated for his work. What dismays me is that it appears that money does not lift his spirits as it does with most men. From observing the way he lives, money is not his desire—it is not his god. If it is there, he will use it. His main concern is for his family, how to hold onto them and to his own life."

"But, how long will it be vital to him? Feelings of guilt may drive him to tell all. The fact that I hold his life and the lives of the others in my hands, may not stop him."

As Yasin put the key in the ignition, he added, "What troubles me more is that we may not be able to stop with the elimination of these two men. We may have to make another elimination in our midst." Tears emerged but never left Yasin's eyes. On the drive back to Boca Raton the men were silent.

19

Boca Raton, Florida

Laila opened the door and experienced an ominous feeling as she entered the empty apartment. She knew she'd be back from exercising before Yasin returned. That was no surprise to her, but her reaction now was based on what had to be done.

She went into Yasin's office, threw her bag on the floor and picked up the phone. Yasin had left Nuri's number in plain sight on his desk. *That man knows me well; I do exactly what he asks. Some day I might surprise him. Why does my mind keep changing?*

Her thinking ended with the receptionist's voice on the other end of the line. "Adam & Eve, can I help you?"

"Yes, I'd like to speak to Nuri, please. Tell him it's Laila."

"Certainly, please hold."

In a minute she heard his voice. Laila's heart was beating so rapidly that she felt it would leap through her chest. Little pleasantries out of the way, she said, "The reason for my calling you is that Yasin's in Tampa on business, and he asked me to have you come over and sign off on the additional expansion plans. The architect left them with us today. Yasin knows you don't want to waste any time."

"That is great! I want to see this construction finished. All I can see and hear is lots of banging, workers coming and going, but nothing ever looks completed."

"I don't understand that, Nuri. I hear from Yasin and Khaled that these guys are working hard. But the important thing is that you sign the plans to keep it all moving. Can you come over Tuesday night?"

"Sure, right after I lock up. I will probably get there around seven. Is that okay?"

"That's fine. You'll only be here a . . . a . . . a short while," Laila said, getting flustered.

"You sound upset, Laila. Anything I can do to help?"

"Nothing, but thanks anyway. I'll see you Tuesday evening. We'll talk when you get here."

She thought, what I should have said to him right now is **RUN!** Get the hell out of Florida while you can! Take your family and **GO!** Take any money you have and fly to Mexico or Hawaii or hide on a Caribbean island. Yasin is about to ruin your life.

After saying their goodbyes, Laila hung up softly and closed her eyes. It was still light and would be for some time. She longed for the darkness to help hide her thoughts. Looking out the window, she saw the waves breaking against the shore. How riveting the water was . . . how peaceful. Her life was in turmoil. And, her head throbbed. She was aware of mood swings, but what was there to do? Why was this happening to her? This was far from the first time she'd been a player in this type of set-up.

Only this one time, she was looking forward to it. She hoped it would not show on her face and that, if it did, Yasin would think she was just a good actress. Laila wanted Nuri's arms around her, wanted his hands fondling her breasts, wanted his tongue in her mouth and feeling him inside her. She was hot for him, but the guilt was becoming too much to bear. Laila knew from his reactions that he was extremely attracted to her.

She must stop thinking of him and get on with what was necessary. Now that the date and time were confirmed, phoning the photographer was next. His number was conveniently placed below Nuri's. He answered on the first ring. "Omar? It's Laila. The appointment is set. Be here Tuesday around three with your equipment."

"I can hardly wait, beautiful Laila."

She slammed the receiver down hard on the cradle. This lowlife would see it all—probably pleasure himself while he was filming in the closet. I hate that piece of slime, she thought.

Laila had to admit though that he was an excellent photographer. His specialty was porno flicks, and he made a fortune from them. Yasin would never replace him.

Taking everything on Yasin's desk and throwing it at the wall was what she wanted to do. But, in the next few seconds, she calmed down by thinking of Nuri—his dark eyes—his trim, muscular body—his touch. Laila knew he was probably unaware of her feelings. The hell with Omar! Let him watch! Let him drool! It was the nearest thing he'd ever get to a real woman.

Opening Yasin's bottom desk drawer, she removed the Scotch, opened the bottle and put the spirits to her lips. She felt her body relax, losing its anxiety. Again her thoughts plagued her. How could she leave Yasin? How could she run off with Nuri? Why was she inflicting this upon herself? A shiver went down her body as she heard Yasin's key in the front door.

"Laila? I just sent Khaled home. I prefer to dine with you, my love."

"Quickly placing the Scotch back in the drawer, she swallowed hard and calmly said, "How nice."

20

The 6:40 AM Continental flight from Vegas to Palm Beach took off on a bright and beautiful Nevada morning. Mario wasn't alert or cheerful at the moment. There wasn't much time between the hour he returned to his motel room and the time he had to be at the airport. Forget about sleeping—he'd sleep on the plane, he thought.

Mario had decided not to dye his hair or change his appearance, thinking there shouldn't be a problem. The ticket he handed the flight attendant read, 'Anthony Luperello', and in his wallet was a driver's license, Social Security card and VISA with the same name. Smiling to himself, he remembered his immigrant mother saying in her broken English, 'Mario, in America if you hava dah money, you get wha' you want.' Momma was right, he'd convinced himself.

A pretty, blonde stewardess stopped at his seat, "Juice, soft drinks, water, coffee, tea?"

"I need a little somethin' stronger than that, honey," he replied giving her a wink.

"Not at this time, sir. Sorry," she said, with a look of exasperation.

"Forget it." The young woman moved on. She's shakin' her ass purposely, Mario thought. Seems tough, but she'd probably make a good lay.

He went back to his bleak thoughts. It was a week since Augie stood at his motel room door. At first he was glad to see the guy. But after hearing the news about Theresa being so depressed—and worse yet, seeing that guy—Mario wished Augie had never come.

His plans changed every minute. The latest: As soon as we land, I'll call Augie, rent a car and get a motel near Theresa's apartment. I wana see my kid again. I love her. She got a bad deal, he told himself. If it wasn' for Theresa's naggin', maybe I might never have pulled that job. Oh, what the hell. I'm livin' a new life now, and grinning, Mario thought, and I like it, too.

ഔരു ഔരു ഔരു

Something else was bothering Mario too. It was what happened last night. Richie Di gave him an extra job. Told him to go to the Ritz on the Strip and pay a call on Salli Ricco. Sal was into Richie over fifty thousand. The whole thing had taken less than an hour, but it left Mario a little shaken.

He'd walked into the refurbished Ritz around 11:30 PM, and it didn't take him long to spot Salli at a craps table, an excited crowd around him cheering his every throw. Looking at the stack of chips in front of the guy, Mario thought: this sick loser is actually winning. After they made eye contact, Salli picked up his chips, dropped them into his jacket pocket and walked over to Mario.

"Wha' you doin' here, Mario?"

"Nothin' much—lookin' for you. Richie Di told me to come here, find you and that we should talk."

"Listen, glad you're here—didn' wanna stop and change my luck. I got five C-notes for Richie. I been winnin'. Can you believe that? Salli Ricco is winnin'?" He looked Mario's stone face. "That's a joke. Why you so serious?"

"This ain't a place to talk, Sal. You got a room?"

"Sure—a great one—on the 32ⁿᵈ floor—lookin' over the big pool."

"How'd you get it, you weasel?"

Salli smiled and looked relieved. "Johnnie Terrazano—you know him."

"Yeah."

"Johnnie got a three-day comp and couldn' use it. His daughter's gettin' married Sunday and probably needed him to sign checks all week."

That's probably it, Sal. So you got lucky."

Mario knew the man was getting nervous, but he never acknowledged it with a glance or a word. "Why don' we go up to your room—have a few drinks from that fridge—on me? And then we can talk. That's all I'm here for, Salli. No shit!"

"Okay, Okay," he said, but the doubtful look never left Salli's face.

They walked towards the bank of elevators. Once they reached the 32ⁿᵈ floor, Salli said, "It's 3207," and the tension on his face started to fade.

Maybe he's proud of the room he's got, Mario thought, as Salli put his key card in the door slot. The draperies were open and the lighted panorama of Las Vegas spread before them.

"Isn' that somethin', Mario?"

"Sure is. But I wanna' see it from the balcony. I'm livin' in a dark, crummy motel room. You don' see stuff like this from my place."

"No problem," Salli said, opening the sliding door, and they stepped out. "Before I forget, here's the cash for Richie."

Mario put the bills in his silk shirt pocket and said, "Sal, we been friends for years, and I hated to hear you got yourself in a mess again. You gotta stop gamblin'. You gotta join one of those groups that help you stop."

"I know that you're a good guy, Mario, and I'm gonna. But I gotta pay Richie off first. And I been doin' that."

"Are you nuts? You know how much you owe, and it's goin' up every day. He's gonna laugh at this five hundred."

Salli started crying. "So whadda I do, Mario?" he asked between sobs.

"Get yourself together, Sal. There's somethin' you can do to work off your loan. Richie even thought of it in case you didn' have the cash."

"I'll do anythin', Mario."

"You see, Richie always got packages to pick-up and deliver. I'm sure you can do that for him. But, don' ask what's in 'em."

"Would I, you lug?" A smile broke out on Salli's face.

"So, it's a deal, Sal. He'll be in touch with you direct."

Mario offered his hand, but then raised his arm instead, closing it around Salli's neck, tightening his grip until Salli's eyes started bulging, and his body went limp. Taking a deep breath, Mario looked at his old friend. Then he picked up the lifeless Salli and threw him over the balcony rail into the pool. Other than traffic moving down the street and the corpse hitting the water, glittering stars were the only witnesses.

No sense givin' this five to Richie when I can use some extra change, Mario thought, transferring the bills to his wallet. Walking back into the room, he used his handkerchief to remove all possible fingerprints. Then closing the door behind him, he wiped the knob and left.

⁎⁎⁎ ⁎⁎⁎ ⁎⁎⁎

Mario slept for the remainder of the flight. During a dream, he did away with one of his older woman companions and he was picking up cash she'd stashed all over her house. He was thrilled until he heard, "Sir, Sir, please put your seat in the upright position and fasten your seat belt. We're landing in approximately fifteen minutes."

Mario decided then he was going to ditch the idea of a fleabag room and get something better. After all the bullshit he'd put up with to get money from his new lady friend for an emergency, he deserved it. He'd told her something about having a low cash flow this month and he had to fly home to Florida—his mother suffered a stroke. He was convinced she wouldn't fork over anything if it was less serious. And before this trip was over it would probably run him a couple of thousand, he figured.

On the final leg of the flight, Mario looked out his window, spotted the ocean, the beach and I-95 as the plane descended to the runway at Palm Beach International. He felt good for the moment, thinking he was coming home.

About a half-hour later, he made his way through a throng of people, his carry-on in one hand and cell phone in the other. He was calling Augie. As soon as he heard his voice, Mario said, "It's me, you son-of-a-bitch. Just landed. Told you I'd be comin'."

"You sure did."

Mario didn't like the sound of Augie's voice. It wasn't the warm, maybe surprised response he'd expected.

"Anythin' wrong, Aug?"

"No, nothin'. Just involved wid some business problems. Shit! I'm glad you're here, Mario."

Now this is better, Mario thought.

"Listen, you fucker. It's six-thirty now, been in the air for hours. I'm gonna' rent a car, and I'll look for a place near Theresa. Gotta see Christy. Got any ideas?"

"Mario, with the traffic the way it is, stay near the airport. You're better off. Phone me after you get the place. We'll get together. Fuck the business!"

"Now, you're talkin'. I'll let you know where I'm stayin'. You're not goin' anywhere, are you?"

"No, fella. I'll wait for your call."

Each of them took that as a signal to hang up.

Mario picked up his expensive, black leather carry-on and headed for the Hertz counter. He glanced at his bag and thought, who says there's anythin' bad about a *kept man*? The gifts are worth the fucks.

℘℃℉℃℉℃℉

The first call Augie made was to Agent Senewski. Although he seldom phoned him, the number burned in his head as if it was branded. When he heard Senewski's voice, he wasted no time. "You know who this is?"

"Yeah, Augie, go ahead."

"Our friend just phoned me. He's at the Palm Beach Airport, rentin' a car, and then he'll find a place to stay. Left Vegas this mornin'. Wants me to meet him tonight."

"Did you tell him to take a place near the airport like I said? I want him as far away as possible from his family. He's a loose cannon. His wife's actions were the bait to pull him in."

"I told him, Senewski, but who knows if he'll listen to me."

"He will; he feels you're his friend. Meet him. We spotted Mario at the Vegas Airport—got him by his description. But we want to know more about what he's doing there besides what he told you. You were to be on him once he came in, and you're not."

"Look, when is this goin' to end, Senewski?"

"It'll end when I say it ends. You're on a thin thread with me now, Augie. Don't break it. Don't ask questions. You do what I ask, and it'll all work out for you. Mario's not the only sleaze we're watching. But he's the kind who's got no morals—none! I don't even know why I'm telling you this, but Mario's the most likely guy to go along with any organization that contacts him and offers big money, plus he'll go on scamming whoever he can. Enough said. Just want you to know you're playing an important part right now."

"Yeah," he said to Senewski, but he thought, who gives a rat's ass about helpin' the government. He's just usin' me and tryin' to make me feel better about being a stoolie.

Silence followed for a few seconds and then, "Get back to me after you see him—no matter what time it is."

"Okay, Senewski!"

Augie was the first to cut the connection, but he felt more like cutting Senewski's throat.

21

Delray Beach and North Miami, Florida

"Damn! Damn! Why the hell hasn't he called? Where is that fuck? He was gonna' call me as soon as he got settled in a room. That was over two hours ago." Augie kept talking out loud and flipping the channels on the TV remote. His wife and daughter were at the mall buyin' more stuff . . . and runnin' up the charge cards, he thought. They said they were even pickin' up Christy, Mario's daughter. Theresa wasn' goin' with them. Said she wasn' feelin' good. When did she ever? Rosie's always usin' her car, her gas, and I'm the one shellin' out the bucks.

Where could Mario be? Sitting nervously on his huge, white sectional, he was ready to smash Mario's face for the trouble he was giving him. Plus, he thought, there was that cocksucker, Senewski, on his tail, waiting for him to report. If that bastard, Mario, had given me a number to reach him, I'd know. "Shit," he said aloud. And, at that moment, his cell phone went off.

"Yeah?"

"Augie—it's me. Sorry I didn' get back to you like I said. Got a really nice room at the Marriott in West Palm Beach. It's only about two miles from the airport."

"So, you leave me waitin' and waitin'. We're supposed to meet for drinks, you bastard!"

"You're not gonna believe this. I get into the room, lay down on the bed, and woke up about an hour ago. Took a shower, gulped a VO from the mini-bar and left."

"But why didn' you call me sooner? I thought somethin' happened to you." Augie was holding the cell phone and pacing the floor. Mario seemed reluctant to answer, he thought. "C'mon fella, what's goin' on?"

"Augie, I just got this one thing on my mind—I gotta see Theresa and my kid."

"What?"

"Listen, pal, I know she'd never let me in if I called, so I'm here. I parked in the lot behind her apartment house. I'm goin' up there, ringin' the bell, and she'll have to open the door."

"Mario, you should have waited. Listen, we gotta talk about how you get to see her. Rosie could plan a dinner at a restaurant or at our house and invite Theresa and Christy. They'd never walk out on us."

"I just hadda do it my way, Augie. What you told me brought me down here. I gotta see her and hear it from her mouth."

"Wait a minute! We can still meet—near where you are. They got great bars in Delray. We'll have a few drinks, get somethin' to eat. There's even a nicer place in Boca—Vic's. What a bar! Beautiful chicks always hangin' around and the food's good too."

"Augie, I don't give a shit about eatin' now or drinkin' either, or even meetin' anyone. You said enough. You don't run me. I'll call you tomorrow. Now I gotta do what I gotta do."

As soon as Augie heard the click, he knew he must call Senewsi at once. The phone was picked up on the first ring.

"It's me."

"Go ahead."

"Plans changed. Mario never called me 'til a minute ago. He checked into a room at the Marriott in West Palm Beach and fell asleep right after. When he got up, he'd decided he hadda see Theresa and his daughter."

"What?"

"That's right. Mario's in their apartment complex parkin' lot now—called me from there. He's on his way up to surprise them."

"You idiot! Why the hell didn't you try to stop him?"

Augie was seething. "I did, Senewski. There was no talkin' him out of this."

"Shit! I'll have to get someone over there to observe what's going on. If that bastard pushes her around, he's not going to know what hit him."

"Senewski! Mario told me he'd call tomorrow. I'll let you know if he comes through."

"That I expect, Augie," he said, furiously.

"Oh, somethin' else . . . his kid ain't home now. She's with my wife and daughter at the Boynton Beach Mall, or maybe Wellington. They can never get enough malls."

"Augie—listen, does your wife have a cell phone?"

"Yeah, who don't?"

"Okay, so call her! Keep them away from Theresa's apartment. Tell your wife that after they finish shopping, she should take the girls for pizza or ice cream or anything that'll keep them out longer. Say you want to treat them because they're doing so well in school or, you think of something else. They're not to go back to Theresa. I'll let you know when it's safe. Get on this right now!"

"Sure, boss," Augie said, hung up and then punched in Rosie's cell number.

As it rang, he thought, I'm gonna ask Senewski for extra money, besides coverin' my expenses. The FBI always pays informers—that I know. This Senewski thinks he can just work me over. I gotta get somethin' for doin' his shit.

"Finally! Rosie, where the fuck are you? What took you so long to pick up?"

Ignoring his question, Rosie asked, "Whadya want, Augie?"

"If you let me talk for a minute, I'll tell ya'. Listen. After you're finished shoppin', take the girls for pizza or ice cream or whatever else kinda stuff they like. Tell 'em that it's on me cause I'm proud of how they're doin' in school."

"I can't believe you're sayin' this, Augie. That's really nice. Sure, I'll do it. So, we'll be home later than I thought."

"Fine, Rosie, enjoy yourselves."

"Am I hearin' you right?"

"Don't make it such a big deal or I'll tell you to forget it."

"Now, that's more like you, Augie," Rosie said before she hung up.

22

Delray Beach, Florida

Theresa, just out of the shower, wet hair wrapped in a towel, was annoyed when she heard the persistent door buzzer. Damn it! That kid forgot to take her key again, she thought. Pulling on her yellow terry cloth robe, she hurried down the foyer. "Coming . . . coming! Where's your key, young lady?"

Color drained from her face and visibly shaking, she tried to close the door against him, but Mario was too strong.

"Is that how you say hello to your husband?"

What the hell could she do? She thought. I'll have to play along with him. Why didn't I ask who it was? I could have kept the door locked, but it's too late now. "You scared me," she said, as she tightened the belt on her robe. "I certainly didn't expect to see you, Mario. It's been over two years and you never even got in touch with us."

"Theresa, I was wrong with what I did. I love you. I love our kid. Where the hell is she anyway?"

"Listen, Mario, we're through. You know it and I know it." Tough-sounding words, she thought. If only she could continue that way.

"Can't we just sit down a minute?"

Theresa knew he wasn't going to leave easily. She saw him looking her over and the lust in his eyes. That was the stare that usually preceded the rape when she'd said, 'No' to his advances.

She'd have to spend some time with him. If she didn't, who knows what this son-of-a-bitch could do.

"Sure, . . . I know you must have come a long way," purposely not asking him where he was living now. "Of course, we can't just stand here in the foyer. Come in. We'll sit in the living room and talk—but only for a few minutes. I'm really not feeling well. And Christy's with her friend and her mother at the mall. I don't know when they'll be home."

"Theresa, don't be so upset. Shit happens, like they say. I ain't here to hurt you. You look like you're gonna fall apart any minute."

"It's because I got this back problem giving me pain again. You know I always had it. It's hard for me to stand on my feet too long, but that's my job. I lost a lot of workdays. I haven't been feeling right for awhile."

"Well, it seems to me like you're doin' okay. This place is furnished nice, and you're lookin' pretty good."

Theresa thought she couldn't be in a worse situation. I'm sitting here naked under this robe with my bastard of a husband fucking me with his eyes.

"What's with you, kid? You're so jumpy."

She thought: Please don't let Antoine phone now. For the past month, Theresa refused to let him come see her and discouraged his phone calls. She'd said it was her back and then her nerves. Then, she'd told him she needed some time for herself. But oh, how she wanted to be in his strong arms. But Theresa wouldn't allow herself to endanger him or his family.

"Anyways, Theresa, I wanna ask you a couple of things. I heard you were seein' a nig . . . black man—goin' out with him. Is that true? And you better not lie to me. I still have a kid with you, and I don't want you associatin' with that kind."

"You got it all wrong, Mario. There's a teacher in Christy's school, who felt sorry for her. She was failing math, and he offered to help; he came here to coach her. If it wasn't for him, she'd have had to repeat the course. She's really doing good now." Theresa's terrified, fearing he won't believe the lies.

"I hope you're not handin' me some bullshit."

"Mario, you know me since I'm fifteen. I'd never take up with this guy. In fact, I don't date. I really never feel that good to even think about it. All I know is work and home. You know you left me with all the responsibility and never helped us one bit."

"I didn' come here to argue, Theresa. I wanna make sure you're all right, see the kid and leave you a few bucks. But I still feel there's somethin' bad you're not tellin' me. I see those circles around your eyes and that's from worryin'. It ain't only your back."

At that point, Theresa felt she couldn't control herself any longer. Weeks of not being able to discuss what was happening at the salon with anyone blew the flood gates open. She cried hysterically. Mario got up from the couch and went over to where she was sitting. Lifting Theresa up, he held her against him, cradling her tenderly. Tears appeared in his eyes as well. "Baby, baby, what's wrong? Tell Mario. You know I have ways to fix things. Tell me."

And she did . . . the whole story, going back to the original phone call from the unknown, foreign man and all the threats made to her. She told Mario about the incident when she had to pretend she was the wife of one of the foreigners—a seemingly nice guy, well dressed, spoke English beautifully with just a slight accent. They'd gone to sign papers in Wellington to rent a two-million dollar house on five acres of land with stables and a tremendous pool.

Theresa started thinking about it again, as she continued telling Mario that it was strange that the foreigner seemed to be mainly interested in the pool and the fact that the area was so secluded. There was certainly no end to the money these guys had, she mentioned. He'd taken her to see the property, informed her that she had to convince the real estate agent that this was the house she must have. When the foreigner took her home, she was too shaken to even go into the salon for a few hours. Nuri, the owner, was his understanding self, as usual. But what was making her sick, she told Mario, was how long would she to be forced to do these things? These men were up to no good; she felt that in her gut. Only a half-hour ago she'd thought, if anyone could do something about removing someone, Mario was the man.

After she stopped speaking, he said, "Don't you worry anymore, Theresa. I'm gonna' find out about these guys; I got my contacts. And I promise you, I'm gonna' take care of them. Write down the names or whatever you got—descriptions of these punks, and I'll get workin' on it. Also . . . tell Christy I'll be here tomorrow to see her. As for you, kid, don't think about them for another minute. These people will fade away—never to be seen again."

Theresa drifted into Christy's room like a sleepwalker, goose bumps all over her arms and legs. She tore some blank pages from one of Christy's notebooks, grabbed a pen and walked back to the couch, hastily jotting down all she could remember from the moment this nightmare started. For the first time since she knew him, Theresa noticed Mario sitting patiently, not saying a word, simply waiting for her to finish.

When Theresa was done, she handed the pages to Mario, who folded them without a glance. She walked him to the door, feeling completely drained. He gave her a hug, put a wad of bills in her robe pocket and said, "I'll call yah." She locked the door behind him. Immediately she felt she'd done the worst thing in the world to tell Mario everything and knew she'd regret it.

෨෩   ෨෩   ෨෩

In the lot, several spots from Mario's parking space, a big guy sat unobserved in a black Toyota. He watched Mario start the car and pull out. Then he took his cell phone from the console and punched in Senewski's number.

⁊Ω ⁊Ω ⁊Ω

Once the door closed on Mario, Theresa headed for the kitchen to brew a cup of tea, and swallow a Valium. After talking to Mario, she was now more frightened than ever. The only good things that happened were that he'd given her some sorely needed money and she'd gotten him out of the apartment. In fact, the hell with the money, he hadn't raped her. For that she had to be more grateful. But who knows what that slime ball would do now, she thought?

The sound of the phone startled her, and she almost dropped the mug she'd taken from the shelf. It can't be Mario; he just left. Damn it! If I had Caller I.D., I'd know.

"Hello?"

"Mom, listen, can I sleep over at Georgiana's house tonight? Tomorrow's a Teachers Conference Day—there's no school and it's late and I'm so sleepy."

"Christy, is Georgiana's Mom too tired to drive you home?"

"No, that's not it. It's just better this way. We were planning to hang out together tomorrow, anyway. So now you won't have to drive me back here."

"Honey . . . that's . . . fine."

"Mom, you okay? You sound weird."

"I'm okay, Christy. Just worn out. Remember to have your cell phone on, and I'll call you in the morning."

"Thanks, Mom. Now you're more like yourself, but don't call too early. We're toast."

"Remember to thank Christy's Mom for having you."

"I'm not a child; I know what to say. Don't worry. See you tomorrow. Love you."

"Love you, too, honey."

While Theresa was talking, she'd filled the teapot, and now it was whistling. Even the whistle upset her. Between the chamomile tea and the Valium, I should calm down, she'd thought. Then, once again, the phone rang and shook her up. I can't go on like this, she thought as she swallowed the pill without even a sip of water. This could be Mario. Knowing him, he'll call me all night and grill me on what I told him. "Hello."

"Theresa?"

"Antoine?"

"Yes, it's me. I had to call. I know you're probably ready to go to sleep, but I can't stop thinking about you. I don't know what I've done, baby, to make you not want to see or even talk to me. I've just come back from tutoring a kid who really wants to pass this math exam next week. Now, I feel guilty that I didn't do my best. I never saw that flicker of, 'I've got it,' come into his eyes. With you out of my life, I'm not focused anymore."

"I told you. I'm sick—the pain in my lower back hit me again, and I went to work with it, which just made it worse. I couldn't talk to anyone. You haven't done anything wrong and I'm sorry about that kid," she said softly.

Theresa's thoughts overwhelmed her. She couldn't tell him the real reason she stopped seeing him was because of the threats made to her and Christy's lives plus concern for his safety also. But, hearing Antoine's voice now did more to comfort her than the Valium could ever do.

"Let me come over now, Theresa. I know it's crazy, but I must see you. There's a reason. I have to make sure it's not what I think . . . that my being black ended our relationship."

"It's not. It never was a problem with me. And you're right. I have to see you, too. It's been too long."

She remembered how wonderful it was being held in Antoine's arms and having him make love to her. She had to recapture that feeling, even for a little while.

"Want some of your favorite frozen yogurt—non-fat, butter pecan? I know a place that's still open."

"No thanks, sweetie. Just come."

"There won't be much traffic now. It should take me about fifteen minutes. I'm on my way, babe."

Theresa put the phone back on the cradle and sat, sipping her tea. Maybe she should put on jeans and a polo. No, she didn't have the strength to even move. Her head was spinning. Just when everything looked like it was working out for the first time in her life, it turned to shit . . . at the job, with Antoine, and now Mario again. All she wanted was a little peace and happiness for herself and Christy. Why was this happening to her?

The phone rang again. Theresa sat in a daze. She seemed not to hear it. After the fourth ring, the message machine took over. "Listen, Theresa, it's Mario. Where the hell are you? You in such a deep sleep you can't answer the fuckin' phone? I just got a connection workin' on your problem, and he'll call me when he knows somethin'. And he'll do it 'cause he owes me. Also, I think a guy was tailin' me when I left your place. I lost him . . . probably a Fed. Now, I gotta get outa here and fast. I still wanna see the kid, and I wanna find out what's goin' on. You're back to causin' me all kindsa trouble, bitch. I'll call you again in the mornin' and you better be home."

Sitting at the kitchen table, Theresa was slowly stirring her tea, when the doorbell rang. She ran to open it, tears in her eyes, and threw herself into Antoine's open arms.

"Baby, baby, what's wrong?"

"I'm so glad you're here. Christy is sleeping at Georgiana's house, and we'll be alone. I made up my mind. I'm telling you everything now. I can't go on this way."

Noticing her robe and assuming there was nothing underneath, Antoine responded, "Looks like we're going to do more than talk, honey." With his arm around her and Theresa groping for tissues in her pocket, they made their way to the living room sofa. They sat down as close as they could to each other, and Antoine covered Theresa's face with little kisses, wiping her tears with his lips.

"Do you want a cup of tea or coffee?"

"Nothing, thanks. Just get down to what's happened to upset you like this. You know I'll do whatever I can to help," he said.

Theresa then lay down on the sofa, her head on Antoine's lap. With him looking down at her, she related every detail from the first threatening phone call, to her having to pose as Khaled's wife to rent a two-million dollar mansion in Wellington. Her story had Antoine looking puzzled for awhile. Then he responded, "Theresa, these guys are dangerous, very dangerous, not only for you and Christy, but for anyone near enough to suffer from what they're planning. They have to be terrorists."

"I felt it, too. It's the only answer, but since I'm involved with them I could be accused of being an accessory. How the hell am I ever going to get out of this mess?"

"I'm with you now, and we're going to work on it. Wait a minute, I just thought of something. I know a Kevin Walsh who's with Homeland Security. I don't know him that well personally, but he's turned up almost every Sunday for the past few months at our afternoon basketball games. He lives in the neighborhood. Though he's a couple of years older than me and not tall, he's in great shape. You'll probably think I'm a nut, but I know he's honest by the way he plays. He never cheats or accidentally bumps someone—he's got no underhanded moves. I judge people by certain standards, Theresa, and I have faith in this guy. A couple of times he's joined me and the guys for a few beers after the games."

Antoine went on without taking a breath, and Theresa, sitting upright now, was listening intently to everything he said. "Just recently, he told me about his job and asked me to keep it to myself. That's all I've learned about him, sweetheart, but I feel we can trust him with what's happened. You can tell him all you know, and he's in a position to advise us what to do now. He even gave me his card. Shit—I don't have it with me. I'll contact him when I get home."

"I don't know. I'm scared, Antoine. They said they'd kill me . . . and Christy . . . if they ever found out I went to the police or anybody else." Then Theresa started crying again, uncontrollably this time. "And that's not all," she managed to say between gasps.

"What's not all? Hold it!" Antoine put his finger on her lips and took her into his arms. "That can wait but we can't." He opened her robe gently; she quieted down and pulled his head to her mouth, kissing him with a passion he never knew she possessed.

"I'm so glad you're with me."

"So am I. I'll get you out of this, honey—I promise. But let me get into your luscious body first. I know you want it, too."

"I do . . . so much," and she held him even tighter against her.

"Wait a second, hon. Let me get out of my pants," which he did as rapidly as Theresa threw off her robe. There, on the sofa, he plied her with kisses, waited until her nipples hardened to his touch and entered her slowly. Then with a strong, steady motion and self-control he brought her to climax. Antoine sensed such a relief of tension in her body that he, too, finally let go, savoring the moment he'd never imagined a few hours ago.

"Oh, baby, that was the best."

Theresa looked up at him, holding his face in her hands. They both lay there for another few moments, Antoine not wanting to draw away from her. Then quietly he said, "Now, we can discuss your other problems."

She looked up at him and said, "My husband, the bastard, is back in town. It's only for a few days. At least that's what he claims, but who could believe him."

"So? I know all about him. You gave me his rap sheet," and then Antoine smiled. "Remember?"

"This isn't funny, Antoine. I stupidly told him all about the threats I got at the shop . . . and what they made me do."

"You, what?"

"He barged into the apartment a few hours ago. I'm terrified of Mario . . . I think more than those other guys, and it poured out of me. He said he was going to get someone he knew to find out what was going on."

"Oh, babe, that fucker knows this, too? That's not good."

"I should never have told him."

"Like I've been saying, you've got Antoine back." Kissing her lips, he whispered into her ear, "I'm going to take care of everything."

"But you don't know Mario. You don't know what he could do. He's explosive. He thinks the FBI is onto him, so he wants to leave Florida, but I'm sure he's not giving up on this. He also said he must see Christy before he goes back underground. I don't know what to do about that either."

"Let me think on this for a little while, Theresa. Right now, try to relax. She turned her back to him and closed her eyes. He held on to her gently."

⁊ಧ   ⁊ಧ   ⁊ಧ

This Kevin Walsh may be just the person we need, Antoine thought. He was trying to feel confident about that but his heart raced and his hands grew clammy. No way is this going to be easy, he told himself. And at that moment, Antoine closed his eyes and prayed, "Lord, give me the strength and wisdom to help this woman I love."

What seemed like minutes must have been hours, Antoine thought as he awakened suddenly. When did they get into bed? He extricated himself from Theresa's hold and closed the door gently. Sitting on the sofa, he picked up his wallet to search again for Walsh's business card. He knew that's where he'd put it but why wasn't it there? After throwing the contents on the coffee table, he found the card—stuck between two photos. He looked at the watch still on his wrist—almost 2 AM. No matter—he'd have to phone Kevin.

Walking into Georgiana's empty bedroom on the other side of the apartment, cell phone in hand, he punched in Kevin's number. After a few rings, he was about ready to give up when he heard a sleepy voice.

"Hel-lo?

"Kevin, I'm sorry. It's Antoine. Something so important, I couldn't let it go even till tomorrow morning."

"If you think it's that serious, it's okay. Tell me!"

"Well, there may be a group of terrorists operating out of Delray Beach . . ." and from that point, Antoine explained all he knew.

23

Laila rolled over sleepily on the spacious bed, her beige silk teddy clinging to her body. The day had finally come. This was it!

The space beside her was empty. She knew Yasin and Khaled had gone off somewhere early this morning. No one said where, and she knew not to ask. Laila also knew Yasin would be home late tonight, to hold her in his arms, kiss her, tell her how much he loved her and how important she was to him. "Look, what you have done for me," he'd say. That was what happened each time she played her film role, and the times were many.

She decided to spend the morning at her spa exercising, and then follow it with a massage and a facial. That should help calm her down and eliminate Omar, that damn photographer, from her mind, even for a short while. She could think only of Nuri—her Nuri—at least he would be hers, if only for an hour. This filming would be completely different from all the others. Laila had to admit she was looking forward to it. By the end of the day she would know what it felt like to have Nuri make love to her. She'd think of nothing else . . . particularly not Nuri's future blackmailing by Yasin with threats of revealing the film to his wife.

Omar was expected at three this afternoon to set up his equipment and probably to taunt her as well. Laila promised herself she'd be prepared for all that would happen. Then she got up, stripped, washed, and threw on her sweats. That miserable headache was back but Laila decided she'd completely ignore it. The exercise should help, she thought, and if not, the massage would. Grabbing a granola bar from the pantry, she opened it and took a bite, then tossed her gym bag over her shoulder and dashed out the door.

ৠ৻঵ ৠ৻঵ ৠ৻঵

By the time Omar was announced by the Concierge, Laila had been home long enough to shower and dress. "Send him up."

At the door all he said was, "I am going straight to the bedroom, okay?"

"Sure, do what you have to do."

At least he had cut out the usual false greeting and lusty looks, she thought. It probably took all he had to get up here. That fat tub should lose some weight. And why should I even care?

Omar's silence was short lived, however. A voice from the bedroom called out, "Laila, come here, my beauty. Lie on the bed so I can get you in focus. You know, this is not the same bedroom we worked in before."

That creep doesn't need to do this, she thought. But she also knew it was easier to comply with his wishes since there was no point arguing with the bastard. As Laila entered the room, in her lime-colored, spaghetti-strap sundress and matching ankle-strapped wedgies, Omar stared at her blatantly from his perch on a stool in the partially opened closet.

"You know, my dear, I usually work with an assistant, but I am obeying Yasin's orders. He said that my eyes were the only ones to observe and film what happens. Obviously he was only thinking of you . . . not to make you more uncomfortable. I am just doing my job, Laila." This was the first time since she'd met Omar that he'd spoken to her kindly. She felt it wouldn't last.

He then added, "And do not think that you are such *great stuff*, like the Americans say. I have seen and photographed far better than you, my pet." Laila gave him a long look and was silent as she stretched out on the bed. "Make sure you show your face and the love you have for your new partner." He looked at her and laughed.

After striking several requested poses, Omar said, "That is it—perfect!"

"I hope so," Laila said softly.

Omar then walked out of the closet, closing the doors behind him, as well as the small opening cut into one door. The aperture allowed him to view what he needed for his filming. Fortunately the huge closet easily accommodated his bulk and his equipment. "Laila, I am going out now. I need to get something to eat, and I will be bringing up some things I left in the car. It should take me no more than an hour."

"Don't rush, Omar. The gentleman is not due here until about seven. You've plenty of time to set up a whole photo studio," she said. Plus eat an entire goat, she thought.

"Why not practice a bit, Laila, while I am gone. Warm up for the scenes. My porno stars do." He smirked and then headed for the front door.

Laila remained on the bed. He knows I don't like that, she thought. What nerve to speak to me that way! She debated whether to tell Yasin about it, but what was the use? Perhaps she'd have a shot of Scotch to give her a little more courage. Immediately after that thought, the phone rang. She leaned over to her night table and picked it up.

The voice that answered was Nuri's. "Laila, my staff will close the shop for me. I can get there earlier. Is that okay? I will probably see you in about thirty minutes or so, depending on traffic."

"Could you give me an extra half-hour, Nuri? I just got home from my exercise class, and I was about to jump into the shower."

"No problem. I will see you in about an hour then."

"That's fine." Laila's heart began beating rapidly. I've got to get Omar back here immediately, she thought.

"See you soon, Laila."

"Right," she said and hung up.

Laila questioned herself. Why didn't I say no to him? I could have made up a conflicting appointment. I could have. I didn't. It's done.

"She jumped off the bed, ran to Yasin's office, pulled open the top drawer of his desk and found Omar's business card. Using her cell phone to keep the house line open, she punched in his number. It rang again and again. Damn! Where the hell is he, she thought. On the fourth ring, he picked up.

"Yeah?"

"Omar?"

"Who is this?"

"It's Laila. Something's come up. You've got to get back now! The guy just called. He had a chance to come earlier—probably will be here in less than an hour. That was putting him off for a little while. I didn't want to start making more excuses and I thought I'd catch you easily. Where are you?"

"Only a block away. But I need to have something to eat—anything—my blood sugar must be falling; I am feeling weak and dizzy."

"I have some chopped eggplant; I'll put it in a pita. You can have a glass of orange juice with it, and you'll be fine, Omar. Just hurry!"

"Thank you. I am turning around right now." Holding his cell phone still open, in one hand, and with his other hand on the wheel, Omar attempted a U-turn. He didn't focus on the on-coming traffic and never saw the cement truck headed for him.

"Oh, my God, NO," she heard him say. Then there was the horrible noise of a crash on her phone and outside the apartment simultaneously. Laila went into a sweat and dropped the phone. The last thing she remembered was falling . . . going down . . . hitting the corner of the desk. Then, there was nothing. She lay on her face on the beautiful, handmade Persian rug, blood oozing from her forehead.

ΕΟ)ΟΆ   ΕΟ)ΟΆ   ΕΟ)ΟΆ

An hour later, because of all the traffic backed up by pulling over for police cars, EMS ambulances, fire vehicles and two tow trucks—Nuri was completely frustrated. Only a few blocks from Liaila's apartment, a police car, with lights blazing, was turning traffic away. He managed to find an illegal parking spot, left the car and walked to her building. It was then he saw the crash scene. When he finally stood at the lobby desk speaking with the Concierge, Laila did not respond to the two phone calls the Concierge placed. Nuri started shouting. "There is something wrong. I have got to get up there!"

The Chief Security Officer, Sid Chait, was summoned. He checked Nuri's Driver's License and displayed a face that told Nuri everything. He was sure the officer was thinking that he probably was a terrorist. All Middle Easterners appeared to be terrorists to law enforcement, he thought.

"Listen, officer, I know this lady is in her apartment. I do not care that she is not answering her phone. She was waiting for me to come up to sign some business papers. I just spoke with her a short time ago."

"You listen to me, Mr.-Mr. Mus-tafa. We just can't let you up there. I know she called your name into the Concierge. But we don't allow guests into an apartment without the occupant being there."

"It is not empty! She may have gotten sick. Who knows what happened to her?"

"Maybe she's sleeping, Mr. Mustafa. Some of these gals sleep soundly."

"If you do not go up with me right now, I will call the police."

"I'm the one who should be calling the cops. You're the one causing trouble."

They both looked at each other seriously for a few seconds, and finally the officer spoke, "Okay, we'll go up there. We'll take a few minutes, look around the place—make sure everything is all right—and then leave."

"That is all I want to do."

"Joseph," the officer yelled over to the Concierge. "I'm taking this guy up to Apartment 24C. I'll call you from there." The two men got on the elevator and looked down at the floor. At the 24[th,] they got off and the Security Officer using his master key unlocked and opened the door.

"Laila, Laila, it is Nuri! Where are you?"

No answer.

He quickly walked through the apartment followed closely by Chait. It took less than a minute to find her in Yasin's office. She hadn't moved from where she'd fallen, and she appeared unconscious. Some blood was seeping from a cut on her head. There were other areas where the blood was congealing.

"Don't touch her!" Chait said.

"Okay, I understand that. I will call 9-1-1."

While he dialed and then answered the questions asked of him, Chait took Laila's wrist in his hand and found her pulse. "She's all right—her pulse is just a little weak. Probably fell and hit her head against the desk. In fact, I think she's coming to now."

"Mustafa, go to the kitchen and see if you can find a dish towel. I want to put pressure on this wound to stop the bleeding entirely."

Nuri ran to the kitchen, opened a few drawers and found some towels. He grabbed one and ran back to Laila. The officer pressed the towel to Laila's head and she opened her eyes slightly. She saw Nuri above her, smiled at him, and then her eyes closed.

"She seems to be going in and out of consciousness," Chait said. "Her body is cold. Listen, fella, sorry to be making you run around."

"I don't mind. I will do anything to help her."

"You did the right thing, too, in wanting to get up here. But I want to maintain this pressure, so could you go to the bedroom and find a blanket or something to cover her? She's probably in shock. The EMS should be here any minute, and then they'll do what's necessary." With one hand, Chait continued the pressure, and with the other one, he pulled out his cell phone and reported the incident to the Concierge.

Meanwhile, Nuri made his way through the apartment, knowing he was more upset about Laila than he should be. After all, she was just the wife of a business associate, he told himself. Upon entering the master bedroom, he saw only a sheet thrown on the bed and what looked like a nightgown on the floor. That won't warm her up, he thought. Perhaps there is a coat or jacket in the closet. Nuri opened the tremendous, carved, mahogany doors, and there before him stood a camera on a tripod, facing the bed, with a stool behind it. "What the hell is going on here?" he said aloud, and then he just stood there, riveted to the spot.

24

At the same time police cars, ambulances, fire and tow trucks were speeding to the accident scene involving the now dead photographer, Yasin and Khaled sat on comfortable chaises, relaxing beside an enormous pool. It was in the back yard of the mansion-type home Khaled and Theresa, posing as his wife, rented a month before in Wellington, one of southeastern Florida's prominent horse communities. Several of the salon construction workers, wearing scuba diving equipment, were diving down to the depth of the pool and then surfacing, again and again.

Yasin turned to Khaled, "We have time now to talk. So if something is bothering you, please tell me."

"There is, and as usual you have noticed it." Khaled said nothing further for the moment. Yasin was equally quiet, letting Khaled decide how to proceed. "It is hard for me to tell you this."

"Take your time."

"I am in love."

"That is something to be happy about, my boy, not to have a sad face like yours.

"It is wonderful, of course. But the young lady involved is someone who might cause you concern."

"Who is she?"

"She works in Nuri's salon."

"That Theresa?"

"No, the youngest one there—Jill."

"How did this happen?"

"It was not intentional on her part or mine. You know I have been at the salon almost every day checking on the supposed progress and speaking to the crew. Jill has been there as well; she is not a hairdresser. She is what is known here as a shampoo girl. Besides her duties of shampooing customers' hair, she also sweeps up after haircuts, so her job is considered more on the lower scale. But the young woman is smart and going to school, learning to become a hairdresser. She lives with her grandmother in Delray Beach." Khaled seemed to falter in his talk . . . and slowly added, "I know Jill is young—she is only eighteen, but quite mature."

That said, there was silence for a minute or so. "Go on, Khaled," Yasin said in a rather edgy tone.

"Well . . . you see, we were thrown together in that small shop. It started with a smile and then we spoke . . . about nothing important. After awhile, I saw the unhappiness in her eyes—even when she smiled. It mirrored the unhappiness I knew as a young man before I came to live with you. I started to come for her every afternoon on her break. We sat in my car or drove a few blocks away to have more privacy. I'd bring her a soft drink or coffee and all we did was talk. We spoke of everything in our hearts. This has been going on for weeks. Of course, no one—at the shop or the construction site would leak a word of this to you—I knew that. I was waiting for the right time to tell you myself and I think it is now."

"I understand, my son," Yasin said in a softer voice.

"After awhile she became to me what Laila is to you. You rescued Laila and did the same for me. Now I want to be her savior. She is young, but she has been through a lot. Jill was associating with the wrong people for awhile and paid for it."

"I see."

"It took some time until I asked Jill to join me for dinner. She looked delighted."

"And where did you take her?"

"We ate at the Holiday Inn in Highland Beach, the usual American food, but there was a beautiful view of the ocean from our table."

"I ordered wine and dinner, and afterwards we went walking on the beach, looking at the ocean, and into the eyes of each other. I held her closely, kissed her, and when she responded strongly, I knew she had feelings for me."

"Did you make love to her?"

"Yes, we went back to my apartment."

The scene Khaled so cherished flashed before him.

෨ඤ ෨ඤ ෨ඤ

Once they were in his apartment, he led Jill slowly into his bedroom. Walking towards the huge bed, they stopped only to look at each other knowingly, but said nothing. Their clothes were tossed aside with abandon. Khaled took Jill in his arms, kissed her deeply, feeling her tongue searching for his. He then raised himself over her so he could kiss and lick every part of her body. He wasn't accustomed to such a young woman. His former lovers were in their twenties or thirties. They no longer possessed the soft, smooth skin he felt beneath his hands. He fondled her shapely breasts gently and then sucked her nipples. Jill reacted to his every touch with heavy sighs. When his tongue reached her most sensitive, moist opening, she cried out in ecstasy. He continued for some time.

Khaled felt himself getting harder. Then Jill gently touched his arm saying softly, "Lie on your back, Khaled, and let me make love to you." He did, hoping to control himself until they could climax together. Jill had her tongue all over him, and then lowered herself slowly so they could become as one. She moved up and down rhythmically—and then let out a moan, allowing him his release—and a feeling of rapture he'd never before experienced.

After a moment or two, they turned to each other and Jill said, "Khaled, I know that I love you, and I've never been made love to as you did tonight. Don't mistake what I'm saying. I've had a few relationships before you, but I thought when it came to sex that all men were the same."

"Why do you say that?"

"Because I've always submitted, and I've seen that they make love only to gain satisfaction for themselves. I felt they thought it was unimportant for a woman to reach the same height of pleasure as a man."

"That is not true, my Jill. You are important . . . very important to me. I love you too, and I have never said that to a woman before. I will see to it that you have your pleasure . . . always."

"I don't care about our age differences or that you're Muslim and I'm Jewish. I just know I love you. You're the kindest, most intelligent and caring man I've ever met, and besides all that, you're sensitive, handsome and sexy."

They both looked at each other and smiled broadly. Finally Khaled spoke, "Can you possibly stay the night?"

"No, my love, I can't. Family responsibilities—a grandma waiting up for me—looking at her clock every minute. And I have to be in the salon early tomorrow. I guess you'll be there, too . . . at some time. And Khaled, I can't go into work wearing a strapless, black dress and these high heels?"

This time laughter broke them both up.

"I will see you at the salon then," Khaled said as he took Jill in his arms, pressing her body against his. "I will drive you home . . . whenever you are ready, though I do not want to release you from my arms."

"And I don't want to leave yours, but I must."

ഇൻ‌ര ഇൻ‌ര ഇൻ‌ര

Khaled quickly glanced over to Yasin, not knowing how long he'd been daydreaming of Jill. Yasin was just sitting there, looking out at the pool seemingly calm and composed . . . but Khaled knew that was impossible.

Suddenly, turning towards Khaled, Yasin asked, "Where is this going?"

"I plan to marry her. I told her that you have a special love for Laila that I have always envied. This is a short time to make such a serious decision but I have no uncertainty. No matter how many women I have known and bedded, I have never felt about any of them the way I feel about Jill."

"This does not fit into our plans, Khaled, and you know how important they are."

"Certainly. I am aware of it."

A silence passed again between both men, and it lay as heavy as their hearts.

"All right now!" Yasin shouted in Arabic at the men in the pool. "Out! Enough!"

They were far from serious when they emerged from the water. Laughing and talking, they removed their headpieces and clowned around like irresponsible teenagers. Standing up, Yasin shouted again, "Hurry! The next group is waiting. This is important business! You are sharpening your skills—ocean *or pool*." His orders were given strongly and with alarming authority. After the last man walked into the house, Yasin sat down, breathed deeply, and said, "So where do we go from here?"

"I was thinking that after we finish this job, it would be my last. I have saved my money as you have always instructed me to, Yasin, and now I want 'my own Laila', my Jill . . . and I want a new life."

Another silence followed. Khaled's hands started sweating as he looked at Yasin's contemplative face. He had no idea what his response would be.

The next voice heard was Yasin's, soft and serious, "I think you are wise, Khaled. I should have thought of that years ago—many jobs ago—I should have considered Laila more and not dragged her through all this for so long. It may be too late for us—but maybe not. First we must finish this assignment, making sure all goes perfectly, along with planning for our future."

"I cannot believe what you are saying. This was most difficult for me to tell you. I cannot wait to tell Jill."

"No, do not say a word yet. I am sure Jill will be ready to leave with you whenever that is possible."

Khaled smiled at Yasin and said, "I am sure of that, as well."

Yasin took on a somber tone. "I have a bad feeling about the set-up here. These men are only boys. Who knows how well they can be trusted, or even this Nuri. But perhaps after Laila guarantees his support with the film, I will feel more comfortable. And this will be the last time she will ever have to do this for me."

"Regardless of the situation we are now in, I think it is the right decision for all of us," Khaled said cheerfully in a voice Yasin had never heard. At that moment, Yasin's cell phone rang; he answered it quickly for there were few people who had his number. "Nuri? You sound terrible!"

The bottom of Khaled's stomach seemed to fall. He knew something bad had happened, but he wouldn't find out until Yasin hung up. This had to be bad—very bad. Khaled watched the color drain from Yasin's face as he held the phone to his ear.

"She is in hospital? What happened?" Yasin asked. Nuri was shouting now loud enough for Khaled to hear.

"She fell—in the apartment—hit her head. We had to call 9-1-1. They took her away," Nuri said.

"Calm down, Nuri. Khaled and I just landed at the West Palm Beach Airport. I can hardly hear you; the reception must be bad here. We expected to be away longer, but our business in Tampa was completed in just a few hours. It was not necessary to stay over. Please, tell me slowly all you know about why Laila is in hospital."

Yasin held the phone shakily to his ear. "Okay, I understand, Nuri. You were at my apartment because Laila phoned you to come and approve some drawings and sign papers. Go on, speak up."

Obviously upset, Nuri, his voice cracking, continued. "It started off weird. When I got to your building, the Concierge could not get Laila on the apartment phone. I knew she was there—I had spoken to her a while before. I told her I could come earlier. She said that was fine—to be there in an hour, which I agreed to. Laila did not respond to the calls the Concierge made. Something was wrong. I must have started speaking loudly so they got a security man. I told him that we had to go up there—that I knew she was home. Finally, he went with me to the apartment and unlocked the door.

"Where was she?"

"Laila was lying on the floor of your office. It looked like she slipped while holding her cell and her head hit the corner of your desk. She was unconscious."

"Take it easy, Nuri. It is not going to help if you lose your head."

"Okay," he yelled even louder into the phone. Anyway, she is in the Emergency Room at the Delray Medical Center. I followed the ambulance in my car. Do you know where it is?

"Of course."

She has only been here a few minutes. I must get home to my family—and I know you will come straight here. Right?"

"Of course, Nuri. Is she hurt badly?"

"Speaking more softly, Nuri said, "There is a cut on her head, and she was going in and out of consciousness while we were in the apartment. I do not think it is too bad . . . but there is another thing that looked strange."

"Wait a minute, Nuri. What do you mean by another thing?"

The answer came slow and steady now, "There is something really odd going on in your apartment. There was a camera in your bedroom closet, and it was focused . . .."

"Nuri–Nuri–I cannot hear you. You are breaking up. We are on our way to hospital. Wait for us . . . if you can hear me." And with that Yasin snapped his cell phone shut.

"Shit!" Khaled said loudly. "I got most of it."

"You also heard me cut him off. But why I did not let him finish is what is probably bothering him—although poor or lost reception is believable. Obviously, Omar had his camera set up for the filming.

"Sounds like it."

"Khaled, now we have got to figure out an answer to any question Nuri is going to ask of us. I did not want to continue with him on the phone as you noticed. It will take us almost an hour to get to Delray Beach from here. In that time, we will work it out. And I will not answer the phone should he call back. I know we will think of something. More important was to hear about Laila not being hurt badly. But this is only the opinion of Nuri. Let us hope he is right."

They walked back to the house together. Yasin paused for a moment and Khaled stopped along with him. "If things had only stayed quiet for another two weeks, Khaled, we might have been out of this mess. Then bringing his head up sharply, Yasin said, "This is our last job; there is a lot of money to be made, and we are not going to lose it."

"I am with you," Khaled said forcefully.

The grim-looking duo hurried in, hearing the young men talking and laughing. Knowing they were getting closer to the big moment, Yasin restrained himself from his usual reprimands. Professionally taught in the use of explosives in Pakistan and Afghanistan, they would be setting bombs on designated Intracoastal Waterway bridges from Jacksonville to

Miami. All were to be blown simultaneously. The reasoning was to instill intense fear in the minds of Americans in every small town and big city.

ഇൽ ഇൽ ഇൽ

Driving in silence along the Florida Turnpike at a steady speed of seventy, Yasin noticed many cars passing him. As much as he wanted to get to Laila, he forced himself to think she was going to okay and concentrate on the other problem. A few minutes later, he said, "Khalid. I know what to tell Nuri and I believe he will accept it."

"What?"

"It really is simple—an opportunity that no keen businessman would turn down. I am going to tell Nuri that my business partners and I are involved with making and selling pornographic films—that we have been in it for years with great financial success."

"Nuri may say that he does not want anything to do with that type of business."

"I will tell him that he did not ask me how I made the money to create his new salon. Did he?"

"No."

"I decided I would be on the offensive. How dare Nuri even go into the closet in my bedroom? And for what reason did he invade my privacy? I will continue to tell Nuri that because of this, I have no other choice but to take him into my confidence. Since the photographer could not arrange for his usual studio, I allowed him to use my bedroom for just a few hours at a price that would make it worthwhile."

"Yasin, I think it is going to work. Sounds like something a money-making business man would consider. Nuri will fall for it."

"I will even go on to say that Laila has always been against my doing this, but this is a business situation where I make the decision."

"Born an Arab, always an Arab," Khaled said. "He knows our men and the supposed power they hold over their women. At least, this is one problem we should have no trouble with, and the hell with Nuri after the job is done. We must keep him silent until then."

"I agree. I do not give a damn if Nuri goes up with the bridges. Our new lives will just begin."

Yasin changed lanes to exit onto Atlantic Avenue in Delray Beach—his hands more relaxed on the wheel and his thoughts now on Laila.

25

Senewski jumped at the sound of his cell phone. He smelled trouble. "Yes?"

"Listen, Senewski. It's Augie. I'm in a ton 'a shit now."

"What happened?"

"Mario phoned me late last night and said that the damn beauty shop where his wife's a hairdresser has got a bunch of Arab terrorists workin' there. I know it sounds crazy, but he wants me to look into it—like I got connections. The only fuckin' connection I got is you!"

"Augie, give me the info on it, and I'll see what I can do. People are always calling us with these suspicions," Senewski replied, breaking into a sweat—every pore in his body spilling out like a sprinkler gone wild. This isn't going to be an easy thing to fix, he thought. Having Mario involved with what was going on at Nuri's Salon was one of the worst things that could happen.

"I don't give a flyin' fuck if Osama bin Laden and his men are runnin' the place. I want Mario off my back. I gotta tell him somethin'. He feels I owe him for what he did for me years ago. So you gotta tell me what's goin' on there."

"Calm down, Augie, you're probably bent out of shape for nothing. Like I said, give me the location and whatever else you know, and I'll get on it as soon as I hang up. It's probably a bullshit story the wife told Mario to make him feel sorry for her."

"I hope you're right."

After Augie reported what he knew, Senewski said, "I'll get back to you in a couple of hours. Meanwhile, sit tight and don't shoot your mouth off to anyone—not even to your wife. A lie can look like the truth if it's told enough times. Stay cool, Augie. I'll take care of things."

And with that Senewski snapped his phone shut. He closed his eyes and tried to think of what he'd do if this was an FBI assignment. After a few moments, it came to him. There was no option left but to eliminate both of them. Head splitting, he popped two extra-strength Tylenol tablets into his mouth from the almost empty bottle on his desk and downed them with a sip of left-over coffee. He started formulating his plan. All he had to do was plant an explosive in Augie's car that would go off when Augie turned the key in the ignition. No problem there—he was an explosives expert.

৪০৫৪   ৪০৫৪   ৪০৫৪

Around two in the afternoon of the same day, after doing some necessary paperwork and picking up a Coke and a ham and cheese sandwich, Senewski phoned Augie. "It's me. Told you I'd get back as soon as I had some information. Mario's wife was pulling a number on him, just like I thought."

"You're not fuckin' with me, Senewski. Are you?"

"What kind of schmuck are you, Augie? I don't do that, and you know it."

"Okay, go ahead. What's the deal there?"

"It seems that the owner is expanding the salon. He was born in Iraq but came here several years ago. He's an American citizen now, but he still has family ties in the Middle East. They tend to try helping their own with jobs and money. On top of that, the big backer is Iraqi, and naturally the construction guys are Middle Eastern. This must have given Mario's wife the idea of making up this story so he'd have something else to think about instead of beating her up."

"So, wha' do I tell Mario?"

"Just what I said. You say your connection found this all out—and you had to shell out for the info."

"Great! Now, he'll owe me!"

"Right! Just to smooth things over, take him out for a good time. I'll cover it. You've been a pretty reliable source for me. Have a few drinks at the hotel and then go for dinner. There are plenty of first-rate restaurants around. You must know some, Augie."

"Sure, I do—especially when I'm not payin'."

"Get the bill and next time we meet, I'll give you the money you spent."

"Sure thing."

"Got enough cash now?"

"Sure, I always carry about a thou on me. You never know. I might see a gorgeous blonde and wanna shack up."

"You're always ready for action Aug, and that's okay."

"For a split second Augie thought, Why is he bein' so nice to me all of a sudden? But the notion left almost as soon as it came and he said, "I'm callin' Mario right now and tellin' him I'll meet him at the bar downstairs at six. I want this thing over with already. Boy, could I use a drink."

"Listen, Augie, everything is cool. Just one favor—after you meet Mario, find a few minutes to get away from him and call me. I want to make sure he understands what his wife did and if he's up for the drinks and dinner. Just let me know that he's not blowing his top; innocent people could get hurt if they get in his way."

"Sure thing. That's the least I could do for you."

"Thanks, "Senewski said, "and remember I can have Mario picked up anytime on outstanding charges. But the big wheels here feel we'll get more info on the Vegas mob connections and extortions by continuing to watch him."

"I don' wanna get involved with any of that."

"Not asking you to, Augie."

"Yeah."

ℜℚ ℜℚ ℜℚ

Within a few hours Senewski had collected all the things he needed to do the job along with a newly requisitioned, black Ford Expedition SUV. He planned to be near enough to Augie's house in Delray Beach to follow him to Mario's hotel and to observe where he parked his car. Senewski was known for excellent undercover work, particularly trailing a suspect. All he needed was about five minutes to attach the explosive to Augie's car, and it would go off when the key was inserted and turned. That would be the last car Augie started.

These mobsters were always blowing each other up. There was nothing new about that, Senewski assured himself. It was a believable happening. As far as their escaping—impossible. Other cars catching fire could happen and then that would be dangerous to anyone walking by at the time. But, that was collateral damage and couldn't be helped, he told himself.

Senewski was wearing what looked like a dark work uniform and had a black metal tool box next to him on the passenger seat. It held everything required. Following Augie was simple. Senewski, sat in his car in an obscure area of the lot, saw where Augie parked and waited for his call with impatience. It wasn't unusual for a mechanic to be working on a car. Hotels often phone for one when a guest has an auto problem.

At 6:20 PM, his cell phone vibrated.

"Hello?"

"Senewski—Mario's okay. He's takin' a leak. We had a drink at the bar—probably have another before we leave. After he relaxed a bit, I said that I found out through my sources that Theresa was makin' up that terrorist crap. Then I gave him the story you tol' me. He wanted to kill her—like he's always sayin.' But I got him to see how dumb that was. 'You're doin' great in Vegas,' I tol' him; 'forget about this bitch.' After we're finished here, we'll head for that expensive restaurant in City Place. Mario said that he'd be leavin' as soon as he can book a flight to Vegas. He's goin' to call first thing in the mornin'. That's what he tol' me. And remember, Senewski, you're payin' for this night out."

"I said I would. Just give me a call tomorrow, Augie, and let me know if he's really getting a flight out of here."

"No problem."

Little did Augie know, Senewski thought, there'll be no tomorrow for him . . . or Mario.

"He's comin' out. Gotta go."

Senewski snapped his cell phone shut and put it in his shirt pocket. Carrying his tool chest, he walked briskly over to Augie's car. He took out his FBI scanning unit, obtained the car code and punched in the correct numbers. The alarm system was disarmed when he opened the door. Getting in quickly, Senewski took the small bomb case out of his tool chest and attached it under the dash with a heavy magnet. Next he took the lead wire and using an alligator clip, he attached it to the ignition wire. Adding to his good luck, there seemed to be no one around and no cars coming in or out.

He preferred this method rather than setting it off himself because he wanted to be nowhere near the scene when the car blew. Senewski was so good at this work that it took him less than five minutes. Afterwards he rechecked what he did and headed back to his parking spot.

ဢၢ ဢၢ ဢၢ

A little before eight that evening Senewski sat on his Italian leather recliner with his German Shepherd, Ranger, beside him, a can of Bud in one hand and his TV remote in the other. He'd told Azhar that he'd worked late on a project and had to finish it for the morning's meeting. She'd looked at him sadly and said, "Jameel is now sleeping, and you did not even have a chance to be with him at all tonight."

"Couldn't help it, hon. By the weekend everything should be resolved. Brought in something to eat in the office so I'll take a break now, have a beer and then finish it up. It's a good thing Ranger never gets mad at me," he added, as the huge dog followed his every step, tail wagging.

"I am not mad at you, Peter," she said. "I love you."

"I'm grateful for that, and I love you too." Senewski then gave her a hug and turned to walk down the steps to his state-of-the-art den/office/game room, where he now sat. Watching television news broadcasts, he continued to nervously change channels but always went back to the local one. Nothing was being reported about a car explosion in the garage of the Marriott in West Palm Beach. Could there be a reason the press wasn't telling the public? He could find out for himself, he thought . . . but then decided to give it awhile longer.

26

Yasin and Khaled drove up to the Valet Parking sign at the hospital and left the Mercedes with the parking attendant. Hurriedly they walked through the entrance to the reception desk.

"We are here to see Laila Ibrahim."

"Room 126," the white-haired volunteer answered after checking her records. Handing them a pad and two ID stick-ons, she said, "Please sign in. Room 126 is down the corridor, passed the nurses' station, on your left."

"Thank you," Yasin said, shoving the stickers into his shirt pocket as they headed to Laila's room. They found her lying in bed, paler than the white pillowcase. Yasin went to her side, grimacing at the bandage and tape covering part of her head.

She opened her eyes and looked up at him. "I'm sorry, Yasin. Everything went wrong," her voice soft, tears streaming down her face. "It went from one bad incident to another."

"My darling Laila, you are okay; there is no need to cry. I am grateful. I do not care what happened. You are more important to me than anything in the world. You will never have to deal with something like this again. Get well, and we will have the rest of our lives to make things different. I will make this up to you—I swear it."

As soon as Laila looked up to Yasin and began to speak, Khaled walked out of the room. He stood leaning against the wall in the hallway.

"Please let me explain. I must!" Laila said, pulling at Yasin's sleeve. He kissed her lips gently. Laila continued, "I too feel thankful, Yasin. It took this terrible thing that happened to make me realize how much I love you—how good you've been to me."

He took her hand to his lips. Continuing in a hoarse voice, Laila said, "Nuri left, maybe a minute before you came. I heard him say that he had to make a few phone calls and then must get back to his family. I was awake, but pretended I was sleeping. Let's go over everything before we see him again because I must know what to say. It seems he found me on the floor of the apartment and had me brought here."

At that moment a mature, short, dark-complexioned woman wearing hospital whites and a stethoscope around her neck walked in. She checked her clipboard and Laila's chart, smiled at her and nodded to Yasin. "So, our injured young lady awakens again. She seems to go in and out of sleep," the doctor said, almost to herself.

"I'm up now, Doctor, and I'd like to introduce you to my fiancé, Yasin Adeeb."

The doctor offered her hand to Yasin and said, "I'm Doctor Kalika Patel." He shook it and responded with a warm, broad smile.

"Your fiancée suffered quite a laceration to her head," Doctor Patel said as she walked over to Laila, taking out a pencil-thin flashlight from her pocket and examining her eyes. "Laila's making good progress it appears. However, you can still request painkillers should you need them," she added, looking directly at her patient.

"Doctor—I was away with my partner on business when this happened and returned as soon as I learned of the accident. What exactly are her injuries?"

"She has a deep gash on the side of her head, probably from a fall against the corner of a desk. That is what she told us. However, it's entirely possible that something may have precipitated the fall and her loss of consciousness. We've run tests, and so far those that have come back are negative, but we're still waiting for more results."

"Fainting is so unlike Laila. She is always exercising—in perfect physical condition. There was no indication of this coming. Or was there, dear?"

"No, none at all," Laila replied firmly, taking Yasin's hand in hers and giving it a squeeze. But her eyes did not match her words.

"Nonetheless, Mr. Adeeb, as I've said, we'll have to be a bit more patient and wait until I have her final report." Yasin caught the doctor's troubled expression and it disturbed him. She turned away immediately and said, "We like to be cautious, but if nothing adverse is discovered, Laila will be discharged in a day or two."

"Of course. Do whatever is necessary."

"Sorry, I must go now—so many more patients to see."

"I understand," Yasin said, as the doctor made additional notes on Laila's chart.

"I'll see her tomorrow," the doctor said with finality and left the room, glancing curiously at Khaled, still in the hallway. He then poked his head in and smiling at Laila said, "I am going to get some coffee. Shall I bring a cup back for you two?"

"No, no thank you, Khaled," Laila and Yasin replied simultaneously. "Go ahead," Yasin said, barely glancing at him.

As soon as they knew they were completely alone, she again burst into tears and told Yasin all that she knew had taken place. This, of course, included the call from Nuri asking to come earlier, which led to Omar's rushing back to the apartment, and ultimately causing the accident that took his life.

"Yasin, I heard the crash and looked out the window. I had just finished speaking to Omar on his cell phone. I was about to shut mine when it happened. One minute he was there in his SUV telling me he was feeling dizzy, and the next minute his car crashed. I even heard him cry out just before he hit the truck. I couldn't believe it. I must have fainted and hit my head as I fell. I don't remember anything else."

"Try to relax, Laila. This will all be straightened out. I will learn what happened. The world will go on—perhaps even better—without Omar if it was fatal."

"Some of it is coming back to me slowly. There was so much pain when I got up. I heard a little of what was going on around me, but I didn't open my eyes."

"You did right, my darling. Let me tell you something important. We are no longer going to have these pressures. I cannot tell you much now, and you are in no condition to understand all I have to say, but you will soon see."

"I hope I haven't caused you too much trouble."

"Not at all. You have only made me see things more clearly. Khaled and I were working on something before your news came to us. Now this makes it definite."

"Can't I come home? The pain is not as bad as it was."

"You heard the doctor, my love. You will probably be coming out of here tomorrow or the next day."

Khaled walked back into the room with a container of coffee, looking first to Yasin and then to Laila and finally going to her other side. He put his coffee down on the bedside table, took her hand in his and said, "You are a sister to me, Laila. My heart breaks for what you have suffered."

Laila smiled up at Khaled and said, "I know, and I thank you for caring."

A feeling of jealousy struck Yasin for some strange reason. He dismissed it at once, reflecting that Laila and Khaled were the only two people left in his life whom he loved. His mind filled with a myriad of plans that could result in their securing the money for this job as soon as possible. But more importantly, the plan for letting the three of them walk away alive had to be developed.

Laila's eyes slowly closed, her hand dropping from Khaled's warm grasp.

"We have to leave, my Laila," Yasin said softly, brushing his lips against hers.

Opening her eyes, she asked, "So soon?"

"We have work which we must get to right now."

"That's okay, my darling. I'm feeling tired now anyway." Her last few words were just a whisper and then Laila appeared to drift away.

Yasin motioned Khaled to the door. "Let us go—there is much to be done."

"I agree," said Khaled, as they headed out, too focused on their thoughts to spot someone they both knew in the lobby. The man was close by but had his back to them. He was throwing an empty coffee container into a trash receptacle and recognized their voices. One man said, as they passed him, "We attend to Nuri first. If we cannot convince him that he was upset over nothing, he will have to be removed."

℠℠℠ ℠℠℠ ℠℠℠

Hearing his name mentioned, Nuri looked alarmed, and then terrified after the last part of the conversation. He turned around and caught sight of Yasin and Khaled as they quickly went through the door of the main entrance. The color completely drained from his face.

27

North Miami, Florida

Senewski's house was quiet except for the low sound of voices coming from the local television station. His wife and son were sleeping. Sitting in his recliner, Senewski's eyes were anxiously glued to the screen. No story about a car bomb was mentioned. No TV news crews surrounded the Marriot in West Palm Beach. "What the fuck happened?" he said aloud. He'd have to call it quits now and get to bed, he thought, and then he felt the vibration of his cell phone in his shirt pocket. Answer it or not? The hell with it! He flipped it open.

"Hello."

"Peter, I had to call you."

Recognizing Kevin Walsh's voice, he asked, "Couldn't wait till tomorrow morning?"

"No way."

"You're not going to believe this, but I have confirmation of my suspicions from an extremely reliable source. He told me there's a terrorist cell operation functioning from that beauty salon."

"That's what he told you, Kevin? You know how often I get that and even more substantial information, and it usually winds up as someone just looking for attention."

"What have you done so far with what I've already reported Peter? You were getting on it immediately, and almost a week's gone by, and I haven't heard a damn thing from you!"

"You haven't heard from me because I haven't got anything to tell you. Just settle down a minute, Kevin. Take a breath."

"But this is for real—we've got to act!"

"Who's this reliable source you spoke to?"

"His name is unimportant. What is important is that his girlfriend is a hairdresser in the salon, and she was forced to accompany one of the Middle Eastern higher-ups, posing as his wife. This was for the rental of a house in Wellington—a mansion with a huge swimming pool—something out of Hollywood, he told me. His gal is scared to death. Her life was threatened! She's a single mother, has a teenage daughter. Her husband left her—he's a piece of shit, a low-life. And he's back, supposedly for a short time, and she stupidly told him about this, and now he's looking into it. Peter, if it's all true, what are you going to do about it?"

"You may be on to something."

"I told you."

"But if you're wrong, this could be a touchy situation. You know I can't take direct action, but I can contact a particular someone if it's vital to our national security. He can be reached at any time. So let me do this, and I'll get back to you as soon as I've got something—anything! It's amazing what these people can track down in a short period of time. That's the reason we can enlist their aid—only if we think it's legit. So give me all you know up to this minute."

After Walsh went over every detail of what he'd learned, he asked Senewski, "How long do you think it'll take him to get back to you?"

"Could be a day or two."

"That long?"

"That's not long. Try to relax—have a drink or take a Valium. They've got to make sure the information I submit is critical enough for them to initiate an investigation. You know that."

"But I'm absolutely convinced, and we're just wasting time."

"I said I'd get back to you, Kevin, and I will. Hang in there for now."

Senewski then heard the click of the severed connection. He slammed his beer can down on the coffee table and started pacing. Ranger jumped up, following him, feeling his master's tension. This thing is growing like a boil on my ass, he thought. Then he plunked himself down on his recliner again; Ranger went to lie beside him. Senewski closed his eyes until the idea hit him. It was obvious.

"You know, boy," he said to Ranger, stroking him affectionately, "We're definitely going out on the boat Saturday morning. We'll take a guy with us . . . but only the two of us are coming back." Senewski went to get a fresh beer in his mini-fridge under the bar, popped the tab and took a gulp. He sat there, and fell asleep for about two hours. Waking with a start, he decided he'd give Walsh some info supposedly received from his contact. He looked for "KW" in his cell directory and hit it. Walsh responded on the first ring.

"Didn't want to wake you, but I figured you'd want to hear this. It's in the works, kid. Just heard from him. There was a discussion on what I gave them—thanks to you—and they feel it's important enough to get on it immediately. That's why he got back to me so soon."

"You'll be involved with them, won't you?" Kevin asked.

"It's out of my hands now that someone really big and his group are taking over. They'll keep me posted and let me know if they need to talk to us further. I could learn more possibly Monday. If these guys are really terrorists, they're not going anywhere suddenly unless they discover we're on to them. We can't do anything rash. You understand that?"

"Sure, I do. But there's so much at stake. Anyone could be the next victim, and it could run into thousands. We don't know what kind of attack they're planning."

"Of course, we don't—right now. What's important, Kevin is that they're handling it, and these men have every sophisticated tracking device available. We've just got to sit tight."

"Okay, but I don't like it."

"You're just too wound up. I've known many guys like you in our business who've suffered heart attacks from this kind of pressure."

"You're probably right."

"Listen, I've got an idea. Why don't you join me Saturday morning on my boat? We're both off, and my wife is great about giving me fishing time. She knows the anxiety I have from this job. Senewski knew it would take a lot of persuasion to convince Azhar, but it was a must that he gets Walsh out on his boat.

"Sounds good, Peter. I've been up for hours, and I'm zonked. Need some sleep. Maybe I'll go into the office for just a few hours tomorrow. Some time on the water sounds great right now."

"And Kevin, if we leave extra early, we can go to Jupiter and the fish will be there—waiting for us.

"How come Jupiter?"

"Had to make some costly repairs to my boat a few weeks ago. A mechanic in Jupiter was recommended to me, and he was much cheaper and did a great job. While I was there, he told me about this area where the fish practically jump onto your boat. I tried it a week or so later. Man, I came home with a terrific catch. Now I'm docked at Jupiter Inlet, but I'll still hold onto the Miami Shores slip in case the fish run out."

"Kevin chuckled for the first time in a long time and said, "My guess is, they won't."

"So come on, Kevin. You're always saying you're planning to buy a boat—like my twenty-four footer—so you can sit back on a deck chair, a rod in your hand and a beer by your side.

And if my contact calls, I'll have my cell phone—so we'll be covered. Come on."

"When I think about it, that's the only thing that could tempt me. I know I'm surprising you—even myself, but I'm going to take you up on it."

"Terrific! I'll get to you about 5 AM. I know the development where you live, and I'll bring food, beer and a big thermos of coffee. We'll have breakfast on the way. I just thought of something else. Can you meet me at the corner of Military Trail and Gateway Boulevard? That way, you can just get in the car and we'll be off. That'll eliminate my having to get through security to come into your complex," Senewski said. And it will also eliminate a record of my seeing him that would list my name and license plate, Senewski thought.

"Listen, fella, those blues bite early—don't want to waste any time," he continued. "And don't drag any rods; I've got plenty. Look for a black Ford Expedition SUV. Just got that issued to me."

"Sure. I'm up early—maybe not that early—but it's fine. And it's no problem walking out to the intersection. I'll be there—5 AM, right?"

"You've got it!"

Senewski dropped his phone on the coffee table, shut the TV off, and said softly, "Ranger, looks like we've hooked him." He then went to his desk, unlocked the top drawer, drew out his pistol, and pocketed it.

28

Boynton Beach and the Florida Turnpike

Kevin Walsh was at the appointed spot when Peter Senewski pulled up with Ranger, seated quietly in the back. Peter's face was drawn, and there were dark circles around his eyes. So far nothing was reported on TV about a car explosion at the Marriott. Other than a few brief inquires on Friday, he hadn't asked more. He didn't want to create a stir; he made no attempt to phone Augie.

"Jump in, Kev!" Peter said in as friendly a tone as he could muster. He was tired—had spent most of the night convincing Azhar that he needed to get away desperately and the last few hours gathering what he needed for today.

"I could use some coffee," Kevin said as he closed the door. He then turned around and gave the dog's head an affectionate pat. "What's his name?"

"Ranger."

"That's a good boy, Ranger." The dog responded to Kevin by licking his hand before he drew it away. Ranger then went back to peering out the window, looking more relaxed than the two men.

"Coffee is on the seat behind you, Kevin. Pick up that red thermos; that one's yours. Made decaf for you, and put my regular high octane in the blue one. There are sandwiches in that thermal bag that should still be hot—scrambled eggs and bacon on Kaiser rolls. Pull one out and get started."

"Got to thank you, Peter. You've thought of everything."

"I try to."

Peter thought: I hope I did. He went over the list quickly in his mind: duct tape, those strong chains he'd saved for who-knows-what, heavy-duty garbage bags, chloroform and gauze, some padlocks, plus a sharpened axe. He had a blanket over some of the things, and others were in the empty freezer chest—the huge one he'd used again and again for a big catch. Fishing rods, tackle boxes, and a small freezer chest filled with fresh bait and another with bottled water were also stored in the back.

"Great day for fishing, isn't it?" Kevin asked, munching a sandwich in one hand and sipping coffee with the other. The coffee was special—a rich, Columbian dark roast with vanilla, hazelnut, cinnamon—and enough Valium to knock out a horse.

"Sure is. We'll get mackerel and blues at least."

"Glad we got the early start. Where'd you say we're headed?"

"Out to Jupiter—the town I've got my boat docked. It's not as crowded as the other spots I used to fish in North Miami. I've had great luck in this area, so it's worth the drive. Got to thank the mechanic who clued me in."

"Boy, this is good decaf. I usually get Dunkin' Donuts hazelnut, but I can taste cinnamon and vanilla in this, too. I could drink the whole thermos right now."

"Coffee is my expertise. It's all downhill from there though," Peter said. But he thought, if the coffee doesn't put him away entirely, I'll use the chloroform. Kevin's not going home with any fish. He won't see fish or home ever again.

Kevin continued eating his sandwich, washing it down with the coffee, cup after cup. "You know, Peter, I can't stop thinking about this possible terrorist cell. In fact, I think I'm making myself sick—nauseous from constantly going over it in my mind."

"You probably didn't get enough sleep last night," Peter replied. He was holding to the seventy mile-an-hour speed limit on the Turnpike. Getting stopped by a cop for speeding would be bad.

"I'm not only nauseous, but sleepy too. Thought the coffee would help, but it hasn't."

"Come on, fella, need you to be my first mate," Peter said, noticing Kevin fighting to keep his eyes open.

Peter was wishing that all this was behind him, but the worst was ahead, he knew. Pulling off the highway at the next rest stop, he drove his SUV into a lot empty of cars and parked. Kevin was passed out now, and Peter felt for his pulse—it was weak. But Kevin was young, his heart was good, and he continued breathing in spurts. Peter thought he could complete the kill with a shot to the back of Kevin's head and then bury him deep somewhere in one of the lonely, wooded areas back from the highway. At the last minute he'd attached the silencer to his personal Walther PP 32 and added a heavy garden shovel to his supplies. He would remove all of Kevin's identification. There were plenty of remote places off the Turnpike.

Someone might find him—or never find him.

Or he could hold the chloroform against Kevin's nose for awhile and keep him out until he was able to move him onto the boat. He'd then bag and tape Kevin's body and put him in the huge freezer chest, add the heavy chains, and throw him overboard. After all he was slight and small—the shortest Irishman he'd ever met. Peter thought about his options, considered the clear morning and watched the traffic increasing.

Kevin looked like he was sleeping, Peter convinced himself. He then leaned over to grab a pillow from the back and put it behind Kevin's head. Now that's a real sleepy fisherman trying to get in a few z's before he went out for the day.

Opening his door, Peter got out and called to Ranger, "Come on fella—let's take a walk right around here. Don't know how much attention I can give you later." Ranger was beside him in a few seconds, looking eager to run. When they returned to the car, Peter glanced at his passenger and knew he was completely unconscious, and would be for at least the next few hours.

Peter helped himself to one of the sandwiches he'd made. Got to keep up my strength, he thought, amazed at his appetite with all that was happening. Pouring some coffee from the blue thermos, he felt himself reviving, ready for the next step. He was pleased with his decision. Even though there'd be no noise, a bullet to Kevin's head would leave a trail of blood behind. The Valium put him out, but Kevin could be kept unconscious with chloroform. When the time was right, Peter could suffocate him with a pillow. After that, he'd hold him up and drag him onto his boat. That's what you do with a friend who's had too much to drink, he thought.

He figured he'd take him below and then go back to get the freezer. He'd throw in the chains and that axe too. In the end this would be a nice, clean closure to Kevin's search for a band of terrorists. He smiled to himself and thought he might even get in a little fishing once the freezer and its contents were disposed of.

Pulling out of his spot, Peter again headed for Jupiter. He put in an old Mick Jagger CD, one of his favorites. Ranger nestled his head on Peter's shoulder. This was going to work well, he assured himself, until he heard the siren and saw the lights coming from the police car behind him. Man-oh-man, what the hell did I do, he thought, as he pulled over onto the shoulder. The cruiser pulled in right behind him, and the cop took his time getting out and coming over. Ranger started barking. "Down, boy, down boy! He's okay." Ranger finally lay down on the back seat, merely observing the goings-on.

"What's the problem, officer?"

"I need to see your license and registration, please."

Peter reluctantly took his license from his wallet and the registration from the glove compartment and handed them to the cop. He started perspiring. The back of his shirt was wet.

The officer glanced at both men, looked questioningly at Peter, and even more so at Kevin. Then he said, "Your license plate is hanging down—looks like it'll fall off when you hit the next bump. One of your brake lights is broken, too. Just let me run these through; it's routine."

It was unusual for Peter to be shaken to such a degree. "Fuck! Fuck. Must have happened when I threw the chains in the back," he said aloud.

The policeman returned, handed the documents back to Peter and said, "You're okay, but you better pick up some wire, secure that tag and have the brake light replaced as soon as possible. In fact, you've got twenty-four hours to fix it. I'm only issuing you a warning, but if you get stopped again for this, it won't go that easy."

"Thanks for letting me know, officer. I can probably pick some wire up along the way in one of the bait and tackle stores. The brake light will have to wait for tomorrow, but I'll have it replaced. Sure don't want someone slamming me in the rear end."

"What's the matter with your friend there?"

"Don't worry about him," Peter said with a swing of his head. "He had too many beers last night, but he'll be up for the fishing. I told him to get some shut-eye so we can stay out late and come home with a really big haul."

"Hope you do. Have a good day," he added, still looking puzzled.

With a sigh of relief, Peter started the motor and then shoved the papers into his glove compartment. He used his directional signal and slowly drove into the moving traffic lane. The cop took off, staying behind and then suddenly passed him, going well over the speed limit. Peter continued to drive in a safe manner. Resuning listening to Mick Jagger, he regained his composure.

ℝ℞ℝ℞ℝ℞

Highway Patrolman Hank Kelly was concerned about the incident. Thoughts came to him one after another: There was something not right about that guy. But he checked out okay— had no priors—so why am I driving myself crazy? Gave him the warning—that's about all I could do. "Damn it," he said aloud, trying to figure out what happened, but not succeeding. I didn't like the way the other guy looked, even though he was sleeping. And there was such a heavy smell coming from the car—something like flavored coffee. Can't arrest him for that—it's not pot. Maybe I should go back. Fuck it! The hell with them! Let them go fishing—I've got to stop imagining things. He stepped on the gas, switched lanes, keeping his eyes alert for speeders.

29

Jupiter Inlet, Florida

"Man! That was a bitch of a job!" Peter said aloud. There was no walking Kevin; he had to be dragged. Then Peter had to get him below, which was even worse—but at least it was over. Kevin was no longer a problem. The sense of relief Peter felt made all the effort it took worthwhile. It hadn't taken long either, and here he was back on deck already.

Peter swallowed a little more gin from the almost empty bottle and knew he should have stopped sooner. Having the buzz made him feel good, no—great, but it destroyed his concentration. The thought that came to him next put a smile on his face: If I ever told Kevin I was on the payroll of one of the most well-known and richest killers in the Middle East, Yasin Adeeb, he'd have died of shock—not from the Valium and asphyxiation. A guy like Kevin would have been devastated. So . . . Homeland Security loses a good man . . . and this bad FBI Agent is going to pull a disappearing act too.

For a moment Peter felt a twinge of conscience. He knew that anything Yasin was involved in would only bring terror, destruction, and loss of life. But if he blew the whistle, his life and his family's would be over. They'd be marked for death. He felt that his job now was to get them away from this mess and to keep them safe. There was nothing else to consider.

So far, my plan is working out. "Yesss!" Peter said aloud. Ranger wagged his tail and looked up at him as if he understood.

"Come here, boy. I'm not the only one who should eat and drink." Peter filled Ranger's food bowl from a can he opened, then he took a sip from a bottle of spring water and poured the rest into the other bowl. I should start drinking only water and coffee, he told himself. Better choose the right color thermos, too.

Peter made a couple of trips to the car, concentrating on getting the supplies on board. He figured he'd stuff Kevin into the chest once it was dark and when he was far enough out to sea and dump him. Peter knew an area of the bay rarely frequented. After bringing what was necessary below, he returned to the deck. Should someone come by, he'd pretend that there was a mechanical problem with the motor. That would be the reason for not pulling out of the slip. Meanwhile, no one turned up; Ranger was his only companion.

He unscrewed the engine cover, placed a few tools nearby making it look like he was busy with his repairs. Peter knew he needed sleep or he couldn't go on. He lay down on the deck, near the so-called mechanical problem, and grabbed one of the loose boat cushions to put under his head. He'd present the picture of a fisherman having to get down and dirty to find out what was wrong. No sooner did he shut his eyes than sleep overcame him.

ᔕᕈᏜ   ᔕᕈᏜ   ᔕᕈᏜ

Hours later Peter awoke to a bad sunburn on one side of his face, and his arms and legs were getting as stiff as the body below deck. He was hot and thirsty and grabbed the first liquid he saw after he stood up. He drank whatever gin was left. "Shit!" he said, throwing the bottle down. He knew he was more than high and had so much yet to do. Looked like Ranger had been napping too, he thought, as the big dog slowly came over to him. Peter grabbed a bottle of water from the small freezer chest, opened it, drank some and then poured the rest on his face. "See, just what I needed, fella," he said as he hugged the dog against him.

"It's time to focus, Senewski," he said to himself. Sitting down at the helm and leaning back, he came up with a quick plan. He'd use his contacts and bank accounts in the Cayman Islands to make his way out of the country with Azhar and Jameel. All he had to do was go to his safety deposit box and pick up the new identity items. There were passports, international driver's licenses, credit cards and cash stashed. It had been quite costly to secure the documents, but if that was the price for their escape, it was cheap. Peter figured he'd tell his boss he needed to take one of his vacation weeks now—because he was just too stressed out. They knew how much he loved fishing, and he'd impress upon them that several days off would rejuvenate him. It was a believable story.

This would give him a week's time to get his family away without anyone nosing around. He'd tell the same thing to that bastard, Yasin. Azhar might be harder to convince, especially with her being pregnant. But having been brought up under Arab customs, no matter how modern she was, she knew her place was with her husband. There'd be less trouble with Jameel. A three year-old boy was always looking for excitement. This was going to be fun, he'd explain to the kid. It could be done, he convinced himself.

Noise of an approaching boat startled Peter. "Damn it!" he shouted. A shabby, eighteen-footer was coming his way. He could just about make out the name, *The Fishing Dick*. Looked like he was headed towards the slip next to Peter's; the space had been empty for some time, he'd been told. What fucking luck, he thought, with all the spots available at Nick's Marina, this dickhead has got the one next to me.

As soon as the man shut off his engine, he jumped up on the dock, pulled in the craft and tied it off. "Hey!" he said. Tall and heavy-set, maybe in his late fifties, the guy looked like he was dying to talk.

"Hello," Peter responded. "How'd you do out there?"

"Great! Best catch I've had all year! Didn't get the big one, but I hauled in a few blues and plenty of mackerel, and they're good. I fillet them, and then the wife breads and fries them up with bacon. That is some delicious meal." He paused in his excited conversation, looked at Peter surrounded by his tools and said, "Got a problem?"

"Yeah, I did. Solved it. Just putting things back together now, and I'll be off." Ranger started running back and forth across the deck, barking loudly at the newcomer as if sensing something was wrong.

"Hold it! I'm not coming on board," the man said, looking directly at the dog.

Peter grabbed Ranger, holding him by his collar. "Easy there, boy, we're almost on our way."

"Name's John Putnam," the man shouted at Peter, coming as close as possible.

They leaned over to shake hands. "Rob Kerner," Peter said. "Got to get back to replacing the engine cover."

"Terrific-looking boat you've got there, Rob. *Fly by Night* . . . catchy name. Hey, why don't you come over here and we'll have a couple of cold beers . . . got some Millers left. Having a real good day makes me feel like celebrating. I'll even fill you in on where they're biting the best."

"Sorry, John—I should get going. It's getting dark, and I've been working on this blasted repair for hours. Have to get out there. And anyway, you know drinking and boating don't mix too well," Peter added, smiling broadly. Seeing the disappointment on the man's face, Peter said, "I guess it's okay for you now—you've pulled in—but, damn it, I still have to stay alert."

"You've got a point, Rob."

"Hope you left some mackerel out there for me."

"Still a few. Good luck then. Maybe we'll meet up again."

"Sure thing," Peter said as he untied the ropes from the dock. Heading towards the controls, he turned around, waved to the guy, started his engine and took off. Almost made it out of here without a hitch, Peter thought. Fuck that fat slob! He's probably had so many beers by now, he'll never remember our conversation.

John Putnam stood on his small deck and looked out on the water where Peter appeared to be making a fast getaway. Putnam, a recently retired police detective, was known for his unusual intuition. He'd made many arrests in his career by listening to his gut feeling. And his gut was telling him something now. There was a strong smell of gin coming from that guy. Beer aside, a gin and tonic lover like himself, inhaling those fumes for years, couldn't be mistaken. These thoughts kept bothering him.

Putnam took out his cell phone, pressed his home number and when his wife answered, he said, "Honey, you go ahead and eat. I'm not going to make it in time for supper. I'll grab a sandwich when I get home. Got a terrific catch."

"Come on, John, you've been out for so long. Head back."

"No, I'm not ready to come home yet. I've got something I have to do first. It shouldn't take too long, and then I'll be on my way."

"I knew there'd be no use in my trying . . . not after all these years. Love you anyway."

"Love you, too, Babe." Putnam dropped his phone in his shirt pocket, untied the boat and went back to the helm. Key in the ignition, he took off quietly, slowly, in the direction taken by *Fly by Night*.

There were only a few fishing boats still out there as the afternoon turned to night. Only the dull sound of motors in the distance could be heard, and a smattering of small lights could be seen if one looked carefully. John Putnam was eagerly looking and listening. He decided to follow the strange fellow on the boat next to him simply because he felt that he was lying.

When the guy said that drinking and boating don't mix, he must have put away quite a few himself, John believed. Besides, he seemed nervous—wanting to get away fast.

Shutting off his engine and light, Putnam drifted along. Taking out his binoculars, he observed the boats around him, but the one he was looking for was nowhere to be seen. *Fly by Night* was probably a thirty-footer or more, a little bigger than most of the fishing boats in that area. If the guy planned to go far, he needed to use his light; there wasn't a star in the sky. He started his engine again. About twenty minutes later he said excitedly and out loud, "I've got the sucker!" There was the boat—anchored. Putnam could tell it was *Fly by Night* by its outline, but the deck was strangely empty.

This was a perfect opportunity to get closer without the guy noticing. Fishing boats passed each other—not as much at night, but it did happen. If this character was below, he'd think nothing of it. What the hell was he doing out so far anyway? No one caught any fish out here. Everyone who was familiar with area knew it was one of the least likely places. Putnam was still a distance away when he shut off his engine, took out his binoculars and focused on the deck. Time moved slowly for him. Watching a seemingly empty boat was frustrating. And where the fuck was that damn dog, he thought. Maybe there had been an accident? There were some muffled sounds coming from onboard the boat—but still no one could be seen.

The hell with it, he thought, maybe I should go home. But something held Putnam there, and he couldn't explain it. At last he heard some noise coming from below deck, and whatever cabin light was on made the person visible. There was his man, and he was dragging a huge bag up onto the deck. The dog followed him and stood by silently. The guy was struggling. "That's got to be a fucking body he's bringing up," Putnam muttered.

ℰℭ ℰℭ ℰℭ

A short time before, Peter realized there was no way Kevin was going to fit into the chest unless he used the ax to chop him up. He abandoned the idea. Nauseous from all the gin, burned from the hours of sun exposure, and not wanting to make a butcher shop out of his boat, he'd work it differently, he'd thought. Figured he'd cover Kevin with the extra large and heavy plastic garbage bags then use the duct-tape to secure them, drag him to the deck and lock the heavy, iron chains around his body. They were quite long and heavy, but even so, Peter thought it would be no problem getting the stiff overboard. They'd need a crane to get him up once he hit bottom—if they ever found him. That was the plan, and he was convinced he'd make it happen.

ℰℭ ℰℭ ℰℭ

As retired Detective John Putnam viewed Peter through his binoculars, he got a good look; the man could be seen clearly. On this dark, cloudy night, the moon unexpectedly made an appearance. It was full and bright. *The Fishing Dick* clung to whatever shadows were left. What was this guy's fuckin' name? Putnam concentrated a moment . . . Rob . . . Rob Kerner—that was it. He watched Kerner as he wrapped chains around the body, the dog never leaving his side. It was taking considerable effort on his part. The sea was calm and quiet; there were no other boats around. Breaking the silence was the sound of clicking. Putnam guessed it was probably locks closing to secure the chains.

He knew it wouldn't take much longer until this Kerner was finished. Something had to be done to capture the thug, but what could he do, he asked himself. He didn't have his piece with him, and he didn't know if Kerner was carrying. The only thing sensible was to call it in. But in those few seconds of thought—something happened. Kerner was attempting to lift the body to the rail, ready to release it into the water . . . but no. Putnam saw one of the chains fall away, and Kerner bent over the body to reattach it.

What was he? Nuts? The fuckin' idiot was practically on top the body. He must be drunk. The chains were loosening, but Kerner was still trying to attach them. It was then that Putnam saw what he thought was the body go over the rail, dragging that no good bastard with it. The splash was monstrous.

Throwing the binoculars down and snapping his light on, Putnam started the engine and sped over to the other boat. His hands shook, and he could feel his heart beating rapidly. Aiming his spotlight directly on the water surrounding the boat, he saw no signs of anyone struggling to come to the surface. Putnam reached for the microphone of his marine band radio and called the Coast Guard.

And on the deck of the *Fly by Night*, Ranger started his desperate barking.

30

Yasin hurriedly dropped Khaled off at his apartment and returned home. He went directly to his office, chose a new, charged cell phone from a drawer containing many, and placed a call to his contact in New York City. When Yasin heard the man's voice he said, "The weather is perfect here. Come down one day next week. Thursday would be fine. Perhaps you can schedule a flight that will get you here around eight in the morning?"

"But, is it not a little earlier in the month than we planned?" the man with the pronounced, Middle Eastern accent asked.

"You will not be disappointed," Yasin replied.

"Thank you, my friend," he said, and both men hung up simultaneously.

It was done, finally, Yasin thought.

He glanced at his desk. Papers were scattered—there was some dried blood on the carpet. Tears came to his eyes. Yasin couldn't remember the last time he'd cried. Laila, my poor Laila. What have I caused you? He was plagued by that thought and couldn't bring himself to go into their bedroom yet. Instead, he phoned Khaled.

"The job is set for Thursday of next week at 8 AM. I spoke with our man in New York City and purposely advised him to fly in that Thursday. I do not want him here. All planes then

173

will be grounded. If questioned, I will say a discovered leak forced the earlier action. Now the real work begins."

"I understand," Khaled said.

"On completion, payment by wire to my account is instant."

"As you say."

Even though Khaled spoke little, Yasin perceived the joy in his voice.

"I am advising our young man next."

"Good," he said. "And then, try to get some sleep."

"Thank you for your concern, my son. But the important one here is Laila."

"You are right, Yasin, of course."

"I will see her at the hospital in the morning. We will speak again in the afternoon."

"Yes."

One would never have perceived that the conversation which just ended was between two men who were directing unspeakable chaos for southeastern Florida, intended to spread tremendous fear throughout the United States . . . and the world.

ഇരു ഇരു ഇരു

When Awad al Barrak's cell phone rang at the house in Wellington, he picked it up and knew the voice instantly.

"Have the men ready for the job—it is set for next week— Thursday at 8 AM. Awad. I will say this only once. We have gone over the work you and each of your men are required to do. Review the plans with the men every day."

"That will be done."

"Make sure each one knows that he must be in his place, on time to the second, and fully prepared for his assignment. There is no room for error. I observed their behavior in the pool one day. This is serious business. If you feel uncertain about any one of the men, you are to tell me."

"I apologize for their occasional lapses, but I am secure with them all as to their ability and dedication."

"Should there be a question about any part of the plan, phone me immediately, and my associate and I will come to Wellington and resolve it. If I do not hear from you earlier, we will see you sometime on Wednesday."

"I understand."

"Very well, Awad. I leave this in your hands . . . hands I am sure I can trust."

"I will do all you ask of me."

There was no further talk.

ಬಿಣ ಬಿಣ ಬಿಣ

Yasin's thoughts raced on. Awad is strong—his leadership is good. He may go far. So, why am I concerned? After this, it matters not. We will no longer be involved. I am bothered though—by something—a feeling that I will not be able to make this happen—to finish this last job and to get away with my Laila—to go on with our new lives.

Yasin's eyes went to his bottom drawer; he opened it and took out the bottle of Dewars, removed the top and drank with the thirst of a man parched by desert heat. As soon as the warmth spread through his body, the negative thoughts slowly left his mind, and he walked towards the bedroom.

The room was in disarray—closet doors opened wide, camera equipment staring at him. Tears once again came to the eyes of the strong, tough man, who'd always kept his emotions tightly in check. Yasin threw himself face down on the bed. Grabbing Laila's silk nightgown, he inhaled her scent and wished this whole thing had never happened.

The phone's urgent ringing jolted him back to reality.

"Yes?"

"Yasin! Jill called me a few minutes ago. There is trouble."

"What kind of trouble, Khaled?"

"She was going home after being at a friend's house and passed the salon. There was a dim light on, and it was after ten, and it's never open that late. Feeling something was wrong, she pulled into the parking lot and saw Nuri through the window. He was running around the place, gathering papers and ledgers and piling them on a chair. Jill said that he looked terribly upset."

"Have you told her of our plan?"

"No. Loving Jill does not include telling her things she should not know. Having seen me there so often, she assumed I have a financial interest in the new building and should be told what she saw. Jill hesitated to go in until she spoke with me. I told her she was right and to stay in the car, turn the lights off and to watch Nuri until I got back to her."

"Khaled, I do not like this. Nuri must have learned something about what we are doing and wants out. We have to speak to him while he is still in the salon. He may have to be taken care of tonight, though that would not be good. We only need him for another week; his disappearance now would hurt us. Phone Jill and tell her if she sees Nuri closing up, she is to go to him and make up some excuse—anything—to hold him until we can get there. He must be stopped."

"I will call her, and then I am on my way."

"Khaled!"

"Yes."

"Make sure you are carrying what may be necessary."

"I have taken care of that already."

After hanging up, Yasin checked for his car keys and then pulled out his 9mm automatic pistol from the back of his night table drawer. It took another moment to find the silencer, which he placed in his jacket pocket. Running his fingers through his hair, he headed out the door.

❦❦❦ ❦❦❦ ❦❦❦

Delray Beach, Florida

Khaled zoomed into the parking lot just as Yasin shut off the ignition of his car.

Yasin waited for him, and together they hurriedly walked toward Nuri's salon.

Are you ready, my son, for whater may happen tonight?

"I am."

As they reached the salon door, Nuri and Jill could be heard arguing. But, all that could be seen of them were their legs moving behind the swinging half door of the storage room. Khaled turned the handle, looked at Yasin and said, "Locked." He then took out his key ring that had a sophisticated, narrow jackknife lock pick set attached. He flipped out the steel pick, used it to spring the lock and opened the door.

Their entrance did not stop the shouting match.

Nuri and Jill jumped as the men pushed open the swinging doors. Nuri looked frightened but asked, "How did you both get in here?"

Jill, reflecting terror in her eyes, rushed to Khaled, burying her head in his chest. Nuri, with an astonished look on his face, stared at the couple.

"Locks can be broken, Nuri," Khaled said, as he held Jill closer.

Yasin looked angrily at Nuri and asked, "What the hell are you doing?"

"I am leaving. That is what I am doing. And I am leaving right now."

"Are you crazy? We have put so much money into redoing your salon into a spa. It will be magnificent."

"I do not care what you have done or how much money has been spent! There is lot going on here that I do not know! And I do not want to know!" Nuri said. His eyes kept moving wildly from Yasin to Khaled, his hands shook and saliva came rushing out of his mouth with each word.

"Nuri, calm down and think," Yasin said, more quietly now. "I will not go into matters that are of no concern to you. We need you to stay here for one more week—then you are free to stay or leave. But . . . there will be no talk of your leaving now, or it will never happen, and you will never see your wife or child again."

"Leave my family out of this, Yasin. The devil came into my life from the moment I met Laila and you."

"Do not dare let Laila's name pass your lips, Nuri. You are not worthy enough to breathe the same air she does!"

Khaled stood quietly at Yasin's side, Jill still holding onto him tightly.

"Damn it! If it had not been for Jill coming in a few minutes ago, I would have been out of here. She must have made up that story about car trouble and that she had too much to drink—worried about getting pulled over for a DUI if a cop stopped her. I told her I was in a terrible situation and had to get out of here as quickly as possible. She argued with me about not caring what happened to her. What a dope I am. Now I know she called you." Nuri pulled over a nearby stool, sat down, lowered his head and was silent.

Yasin drew up another stool and sat beside him, saying softly, "I am a man of my word, Nuri; you will have to believe me. I swear to you that your wife and daughter will be killed before your eyes—your daughter first, so that you both will see it. Your wife and then you will follow if you do not obey me."

Nuri's face, torn with emotion, appeared to have aged years in the time it took Yasin to make the threat.

Khaled motioned Jill to sit on one of the cartons holding supplies, which she did, keeping her eyes on him. Although he said nothing, Khaled made sure Nuri observed the pistol he removed from his jacket along with the silencer immediately attached. He didn't take aim, but kept it at his side.

Once again Yasin spoke in a comforting tone. "Nuri, whatever reasons you have for wanting to discontinue our contract, I care not to know. I have enough problems. Laila is still in hospital, and I will not allow you to complicate my life further. One week for you to continue as you were in this salon is all I ask. You can go home now, if you agree to act as if nothing happened. Or if you do not, your wife and child will be brought here."

"How can I go home now and pretend that nothing has happened? I have already asked my wife to pack as little as we need for some days on the road. I am taking whatever cash I have and heading away from here. I do not know what made me decide to take my ledgers and a few other business and personal papers. I just wanted to save our lives," he said. I made a terrible mistake, he thought. If only I had taken the cash and gone.

"If you listen to me, you will be fine, Nuri. Your wife and daughter will not be touched. One more week will change things for us all—for the better. Do not make me repeat what I just told you."

Nuri broke down and cried—shielding his face with his hands. "How can one Arab be so vile against another?" he shouted.

"You must not cry before a woman, Nuri. A man is too strong to do that."

Nuri did not look up. He was crying because he knew he could kill Yasin with his bare hands. His anger gave him the strength of more than one man; he felt he could pull Yasin's arms and legs from their sockets and take out his heart with his fingers. But he was well aware that he had to restrain himself. He cried for his wife and little girl. Nuri realized Khaled would shoot him before he could kill Yasin. And then what?

He made up his mind. His wife should be ready to go— they would all leave as soon as he got home. Fuck Yasin! How can I believe anything he says?

Jill no longer looked at Khaled, but focused her attention on an opened wall safe, which she never knew existed. Then she stared at the men watching Nuri.

Wiping his face with his shirtsleeve, Nuri said, "I have no choice. I will do it—I will do as you say, Yasin, but not for more than a week. You have my promise."

Khaled unscrewed the silencer from his gun and put both away.

Jill caught Khaled's eye and her look and hunched shoulders seemed to say: What the hell am I doing? How did I get involved with these people? Should I leave? Will they let me go?

Khaled returned her look and shook his head ever so subtly, no.

31

West Palm Beach, Florida

Unsteady on his feet, Mario could hardly make it out of Morton's Steak House after dinner. He laid a hand on Augie's shoulder as they waited for the valet to bring the car. *They should have been dead.*

"I think you had one too many Old Fashioneds, my friend," Augie said.

"You're right. But I feel great . . . and you're drivin' me back to the hotel, so who gives a shit?"

ℬℭ ℬℭ ℬℭ

Set to go off when Augie placed the key in and turned on the ignition, the bomb Senewski planted in the car in Marriot's parking lot, failed. Senewski had taken the lead and ignition wires and attached them to each other with a strong alligator clip. But the clip had snapped off as Senewski slammed Augie's car door.

Unknown to Senewski was that the manufacturer of these once-so-dependable, nickel-plated alligator clips recalled this particular model months before. So many cases were reported where the faulty clips had fallen apart that the firm was issuing full refunds on return.

All the explosive materials were still in Augie's car. The clip parts had fallen behind the floor mat and the wires hung loosely. The bomb case was still securely attached under the dash. Augie and Mario were unaware of how lucky they were to be alive. With Augie's anguished thoughts and Mario's drunkenness, no notice was taken. They had simply gotten in and Augie drove to the restaurant and left the car with the valet.

෨෦ඥ   ෨෦ඥ   ෨෦ඥ

Now, as they waited for the car's return, Mario was softly singing, "I've Got the World on a String," one of his favorite Frank Sinatra ballads, while Augie went over the evening in his mind. He was not pleased with the way dinner went. The drinks, the filet-mignon steaks were terrific and even that creamed spinach was good. But listening to Mario talk about maybe remaining in Florida, dropping the old babe he'd set up in Vegas, upset him. Mario had said, "Plenty of old, rich bitches here in Palm Beach lookin' for sex, right Augie?"

Augie had agreed with him. What else could he do? Now, they were silent though Augie was deep in thought.

He didn't need this. Augie had that FBI schmuck, Senewski, and this bastard, Mario, pressuring him and not leaving him alone. He was in the middle. He felt the hold they had on him would never end unless he took them both out. First, he had to get rid of Mario and fast. Then, he'd work on Senewski.

The valet drove the car up to them and Augie pushed Mario into the passenger seat as soon as the door was opened. As the valet ran around to the driver's side to get the door, Augie handed the kid a ten just to get his surprised look, his "Thanks," and the big grin. Might as well make somebody happy tonight.

He knew he was a little high, but glad he'd nursed his drinks. They made a generous Old Fashioned—didn't skimp on the rye. If he weren't driving, he'd have considered ordering more—especially since the night was on Senewski. Fuck the meal and the drinks, he told himself; he had to figure out how to bump off Mario. And now, the nut was singin' a slurred but louder version of "All or Nothin' at All." Mario always said he was another Sinatra, and he wasn't bad, Augie thought.

"Put one of Frank's CDs in, Aug, I know you got 'em."

"Sure." Better to have him singin' so I'll have a chance to think. He inserted the "Fly Me to the Moon" album from the CD case next to him.

"Now, that's my boy," Mario said and went on to sing "My Way" along with Sinatra.

The CityPlace area in West Palm Beach was going through a tremendous amount of construction, and Augie was constantly seeing detour signs. There were few lights and no traffic where he'd just turned, and looking at the rubble-filled sites gave him the idea. "I think I'm gettin' a flat, Mario. I feel it. I'm pullin' over to check it out."

Mario, still singing, louder now, didn't respond. Only when the car lurched over the sidewalk, going up into the construction area and pulling out of sight of the street, did Mario comment. "Augie, what the fuck you doin'?"

"Told you—gotta check the tires. I know one's flat. It'll be easier to change it here than in the street."

Augie took a flashlight from the glove compartment, pressed the button on his key, flipping the trunk lid open, and got out of the car. He left his door ajar and the motor running. "Shit!" he shouted, as he bent down, supposedly examining the tire, while actually using his flashlight to look around. He spotted yellow CAUTION tape attached to barriers, surrounding an area. Figuring if they'd blocked off that space, it probably was open and dangerous. Augie then pulled the trunk lid up and took out his jack handle—holding it behind him.

"Mario, get out here!" he shouted. "I need help. I gotta change it. The air's almost all gone. I'm drivin' on the rim. Just hold the fuckin' flashlight."

With Sinatra still singing, Mario stumbled out of the car, made his way over to Augie. "Listen, Aug, I'm in no condition to give yah a hand. I'm out of it. I kin hardly stand."

Augie took a few steps back and holding the jack handle in both hands, he raised it and came down on Mario's head. The man was dead before he hit the ground.

"Damn it!" he said aloud and thought, what a schmuck! Didn't realize I'd get all this blood over me, but he calmed down quickly when he remembered the old sweat suit he kept in the trunk.

Wasting no time, Augie dragged the heavy body to what actually turned out to be a deep excavation, surrounded by that yellow tape.

No traffic, no people . . . perfect, he thought.

Before dropping Mario down the hole, he removed his wallet and took out the credit cards and cash. Figured he'd get rid of the wallet later. He even took off the gold chains Mario was wearing and his diamond pinky ring. Feeling satisfied, he put the jewelry in his pants pockets. There'd be no way to easily identify the body. Augie had it worked out. The cops will see that he was drunk, probably dropped off nearby, got lost, robbed, slammed by some local gang and then thrown down here.

‽‽‽ ‽‽‽ ‽‽‽

At the same time Augie and Mario had been waiting for the car at Morton's, three teenagers had walked from Pleasant City to CityPlace, never knowing that their paths would cross. Two of the young men had been outside their neighborhood convenience store when they spotted the third, Sharim Williams. He was walking out of his house smoking a cigarette and heading in the opposite direction. Anthony Hodges, over six feet tall, had a physique like a heavyweight boxer. He had a gold-toothed smile and dreadlocks, and it was known that people rarely said *No* to him.

"Yo, Sharim! College Boy, Church Boy, what y'all doin' smokin'?"

"Yeah, man," his well-known echo, Jamal Miley, tall, thin, shaved head, four gold studs in one ear, said. "C'mon ovah."

Sharim stopped and turned to the two. He was tired of being teased by these one-time friends whom he no longer considered his friends. They were high school drop-outs and members of the Black Warriors. They didn't leave him be. Sharim was not in any gang. He was in line for a scholarship at Howard University in Washington, D.C. and only had a few months to go before he'd be on his way. He was the youngest of five. His father had taken off years ago; they'd never heard from him. His mother, a nurse's aide, worked during the week at JFK Hospital and on weekends in the Delray Medical Center. He knew she wanted that scholarship for him more than he did.

But if it wasn't for his Uncle Antoine, a teacher at Delray Beach High School, who encouraged and tutored him, he might never have had a chance. A few years ago, feeling deprived and mad at the world, he was ripe, just as his friends were, perfect for gang membership. It was his uncle who'd stepped up and talked him out of it and Sharim loved and respected him for it.

"We askin' you to come over, Sharim. Hang with us for awhile," Anthony said.

Trying to hide his reluctance, he crossed the street and slowly walked over to them.

"Listen, Bro, we aimin' to take a walk to CityPlace . . . see what we can see," said Anthony, smiling.

"Yah, Sharim, you been actin' too good for us," added Jamal.

No way did Sharim want to join them, but this time he couldn't bring himself to say no. He'd already told his mother he'd be out for awhile—thinking then of a solitary walk—have a few smokes and call it a night. But Sharim answered with a soft, "Sure, man. I'll hang with you for awhile."

They walked and jostled each other. And when they saw an empty soda can in the gutter, they kicked it down the block like they did when they were kids. Sharim was beginning to feel a little better about them. He remembered how much fun they had together before they grew up. That feeling didn't last for long.

When the trio reached the construction area, they were near the spot where Augie had left his car—still running. Anthony piped up with, "We stoppin' right here. I hear a motor." As they walked toward the sound, he saw it—an empty Caddy.

"Man this car was just callin' out to me."

"You right, Bro," Jamal chimed in.

"I don't think it's such a good idea. This is a construction site. Maybe it's the security man's car and he's just checking on something, and he'll be right back. He may have a gun," Sharim said—his voice cracking.

"College Boy, you sure don't wanta take any chances—do you now? A night security guy with a new Caddy? Are you crazy, man?" Jamal asked, glaring at Sharim.

Anthony quickly shoved Sharim aside and headed towards the car with Jamal lagging behind. Sharim stood frozen to the spot. It was as if they were in a world by themselves. Not a sound came from the street.

Then Sharim spoke. "Shit! I'm leaving. Don't want no part of this," but before he could turn and go, he saw a big white guy running towards them. It was Augie—out of breath and shouting. "Get the hell away from my car, you fuckin' bastards!" Then he pulled a .45 from his pocket, pointing it at Anthony.

We jus' lookin' at it. Not doin' a thing," Anthony said.

Jamal quietly slipped into the shadows behind Augie and picked up a broken two-by-four. He slammed Augie's head with it so hard that the sound of the blow filled the air like the crack of a bat bringing in a home run.

"That's it! I'm out of here." Sharim said, the first to speak.

"You ain't goin' nowhere, Sharim. You in this with us," Anthony said, and then continued, "First, shut off that motor and that fuckin' radio, Sharim. And Jamal, just don't stand there staring. You seen a dead man befo."

"Not one I just killed," he said. Augie's blood covered Jamal's face, shirt and pants.

"Shut yah mouth, Jamal, and look in his pockets for cash and credit cards."

"Sharim, you take his bling, but don't cop his cell. That fuckin' phone could bring us all kinds of trouble, Bro."

"I'm gonna look for a place to dump him. Looks like that's no problem 'round here."

"Anthony, hold it. I don't want to be mixed up with what happened. You know I'd never talk. Let me walk away . . . please!" Sharim said.

"Listen, man, you see this bloody piece of wood? It's still strong enough to knock you off, too. Understand?"

Sharim nodded and looked down at the ground.

Anthony walked away quickly towards the rear of the area.

Jamal, on one knee, said, "Man, look at this! Two wallets—more jewelry—cash and credit cards. We done hit the jackpot tonight, Bro, and we got his piece, too." He stared at the collection on the ground beside him, the look of shock never leaving his face.

Anthony, making his way back was shouting, "Let's get the hell outa here! I could make out another stiff in that hole I found. Jamal! Throw this guy in there too, and we're gone! But wait a minute—got all his stuff?"

"Sure do—and there's enough for a lotta weed and even pure white powder, man."

"Sharim! Did you strip all the jewelry he was wearing and then give it to Jamal?"

"I did," Sharim answered softly, not even looking at Anthony.

"There was even more gold in his pockets . . . I can't believe it. Tell me this ain't no dream," Jamal said.

"Okay, man, enough carryin' on. Take care of this body. Jus' keep walkin' towards the back and you'll see the hole; it's close. There's a small light coming from a CAUTION barrier around it."

Jamal lifted Augie's body easily and headed the way he was directed.

"Get in the car, Sharim," Anthony said.

Anthony got behind the wheel, but didn't put on the lights. Jamal returned shortly—puffing away. Not one word passed between Anthony and Sharim.

"Hey, what's wrong with you two? Jamal glanced back at Sharim. "Our homey lost his cool?" he asked.

Still, there was no response from Sharim.

Anthony backed out of the area quietly and put the lights on. Jamal, beside him, looked again at the gold necklaces, bracelets, rings and then at the credit cards. After he carefully counted the cash, utilizing whatever light there was from the instrument panel, he shoved everything in his pockets. Then, he put the wallets and the gun in the glove compartment.

"What a night," Jamal said. We get cash, credit cards, real cool gold, a Caddy and a piece, too! Man!"

Sharim had not looked up since he entered the car.

"Hey, Sharim, we're splittin' three ways. Don't get so fuckin' mad at us," Anthony shouted as he pressed his foot down harder on the gas pedal. He made it quickly through the local streets and entering onto the Florida Turnpike, he said, "Look at that—this car has a Sun Pass, too—we don't pay no tolls neither." That remark brought laughter and back slapping from Jamal. Anthony was hitting seventy–then eighty.

Sharim still had not said a word; he sat there, head up now, staring into space.

"Where we headin'?" Jamal asked.

"Goin' to Pompano Beach, around 31ˢᵗ Avenue. I got connections there. Boy, we goin' be high tonight—and on the good stuff."

"Hey, Anthony, what about all this damn blood on me?"

"You don't have to get outta the car, my man. I'll score the weed and rocks. And if anyone sees you and asks, say you got into a fight with a mean brother. Takin' one look at you, Jamal, they gotta believe that."

They both laughed this time and looked back at Sharim who didn't move a muscle. "We not lettin' that white-speakin' Oreo spoil our good time, are we, Jamal?"

"No suh!" Jamal replied.

A few seconds later, they heard the screech of a siren and saw flashing lights behind them.

"I shoulda kept to the speed, man, but I ain't gonna stop, Jamal."

"You right. You can shake those cops with this Caddy . . . no sweat. As soon as we lose them, just turn this baby off the road and we bail out. Hate to give it up, man, but we gotta. We gotta run, too. Remember we was the runnin' champs in school."

"Yeah, Jamal. But don't talk no more. Look for a good place . . . shrubs . . . anything to give us some cover. If those cops get us, we're fried."

Anthony pushed the pedal down to the floor, going over a hundred, with the police cruiser following. The few cars in front of them were pulling off to the shoulder.

It was then Sharim decided he was going to jump out, and he moved as close as he could to his door. And here was his chance, he thought. A flashing yellow light attached to a sign read: Road Work Ahead–1,000 feet, and then another sign followed, showing two lanes going into one.

"Shit! We caught up with the traffic. It's slowin' down because of that fuckin' construction ahead."

"Go around it on the shoulder," Jamal shouted.

"Tryin', man."

And that's all that Sharim needed. He opened the door of the car that was now moving slower, fought the wind pushing it closed, jumped out onto the dark highway—feeling the pain of each bump as he rolled over and over. He finally hit an embankment and landed in a muddy, swamp area, overflowing with water because of the recent heavy rains. The speed of the car had propelled his body rapidly. He was sinking. I'm just going to let myself go down, he thought. I've ruined my life, Momma's and Uncle Antoine's. This is the only way I can save them more grief, he thought, as the mud started filling his mouth and covering his eyes. But just before he took what might have been his last breath, he forced himself up, and unknown to him until he made the attempt, found the swamp was only a few feet deep. Coughing and spitting out mud, he made his way slowly to the embankment.

"Fuck them!" he thought—those losers aren't going to make me give up everything. No! Not after I've come this far. Barely able to walk, limping, breathing heavily, covered with slime, bruised and bleeding, Sharim made his way to the edge of the highway. He saw more police cruisers speeding by, lights flashing and sirens blasting. The last one screeched to a stop yards away from him, pulled off onto the shoulder and backed up.

"What happened to you, kid?" the burly copy asked as he opened his door and got out.

"I fell into that ditch over there," Sharim said, speaking hoarsely, wiping his muddy mouth with his somewhat cleaner hand and then pointed to the area he'd just left.

"Got to be more than that. What's your name?"

He coughed out a low, "Sharim Williams."

"Sit down on the ground here, Sharim, before you fall down," the officer said. To his partner, he shouted, "Call for an ambulance and then get a blanket out here, Mike. This fella needs help. He's shivering and covered with all kinds of shit."

Sharim was sitting, his head in his hands, when the other cop came over and wrapped a blanket around him.

"Thanks, Mike. We're on this now. They got enough cars going after that fuckin' Caddy to capture an army.

"You're damn right," his partner responded.

"We'll call it in." Glancing at Sharim, he said, "Just rest there, kid. EMS should be here in a few minutes."

Sharim closed his eyes, but he was fully aware of what the officers were saying to each other, though he had to strain to hear them.

"This fella was not out for a hike on the Turnpike and just fell into that swamp," the first officer said to the other.

"You're right, Ed, but it's going to be awhile before he's ready for questioning. I don't know how you spotted him. I had no idea what the hell you were pulling over for."

"I saw him for a split second. Looks more injured than what he'd get from a fall in a ditch. Probably involved with that damn chase—must be a stolen car. Too coincidental for him to just be here."

Mike headed for the cruiser, saying, "If he's in on it, we'll get it out of him."

Sharim was thinking perhaps it would have been better if he'd let himself sink.

32

Boca Raton and Delray Beach, Florida

Drinking his coffee before leaving for the hospital, Yasin turned the pages of the day's Sun Sentinel and spotted a small headline on the bottom of page three in the Local section:

Body of FBI Agent Found in Jupiter Inlet. *A Coast Guard cutter called into service discovered the dead body of Peter Senewski, an Agent with the FBI in Miami. He was picked up early this morning floating in the Bay. A local fisherman, retired Police Detective John Putnam, returning from a fishing trip late yesterday, alerted the Coast Guard that he'd seen a man described as Senewski struggling to throw what appeared to be a chained body, overboard. Putnam said the man seemed to be entangled with the body he held and both went over into the water. Identification of Senewski was made by his wife. The body is being held by the Medical Examiner's Office until an autopsy is performed to determine the cause of death. The search in and around Jupiter Inlet continues.*

Yasin felt his body shiver when he spotted Senewski's name. Everything was unraveling, but what did it matter? He was better off having less to concern himself with, he thought. It should take far more than a week, if ever, to find any connection between Senewski and himself. Yasin needed even less than that. There was only one thought he could focus on this minute—getting Khaled out of Florida to a safe place and Jill with him, if that was what he wanted. Yasin phoned him.

"Our friend Peter is in the Sun Sentinel today. He was found dead in Jupiter Inlet. It appeared at the bottom of page three in the Local section. It is probably on the front page of the Miami Herald."

"I did not notice it, but I will look now."

"Khaled—that can wait. It has no bearing on our plans. But you and Jill must leave as soon as possible. New passports should be made up for both of you in the next few hours. I assume Jill does not have one.

"You are right."

"Then, if there is time only to make one, it will have to be for Jill. You will have to use the one you carry. I would have preferred it to be clean of countries stamped, but we have no other choice. You know who to go to for that, my boy, and whatever they ask for, pay them without discussion. Make sure you have enough cash. Conserving time right now is more important than money."

"I will do as you say, but why this sudden hurry?"

"Please, Khaled—have I ever given you wrong advice?"

"Never. I will get started at once."

"Make sure that Jill tells her grandmother something that will keep her from calling the police to report her granddaughter missing."

"Jill will do it."

"Take minimal luggage. You can buy everything you need once you get to your final destination. I suggest you look into any possible way of getting out of Florida that will be short and preferably hard to identify. Laila and I will join you sometime later."

"Why not now?"

"There are still matters I must resolve, and it will be safer if we travel separately."

ೞେ౪　ೞେ౪　ೞେ౪

Yasin walked into the lobby of the Delray Medical Center carrying a small suitcase and headed for the hallway to Laila's room without stopping for his Visitor's I.D. He was in such a hurry that he almost collided with Doctor Panje.

"Mr. Adeeb," she exclaimed.

Yasin looked surprised at her remembering him. He was used to most Americans forgetting his name, but she was an immigrant.

"Doctor Panje! My apologies."

Yasin always recalled the names of people who were important to him, and Laila's doctor was certainly one.

"It's quite all right. I'm glad I have to talk to you before you visit with Laila."

"Has her condition changed? For the worse? I am ready to take her out of here today—I have brought her clothes."

"Let's sit down in the lobby for a few moments. I have to tell you something about Laila's condition," Doctor Panje said softly.

"Of course, tell me, please," Yasin said at they chose seats in a less occupied area.

"Mr. Adeeb, are you familiar with the word, aneurysm?"

"Somewhat. I know it is a bulge that develops in a blood vessel. Unfortunately, I had a good friend who died of one suddenly. He never knew he had it. Is that what Laila has?" Yasin asked, color draining from his face.

"Calm yourself, Mr. Adeeb. Yes, Laila does have an aneurysm, but the good news is that we've discovered it. If it's at all possible to treat, we'll do so. She is young and basically strong. There are two ways of handling this through surgery, and we will decide which one will be better for her. However, most aneurysms can be tricky and hers is no different. She has what is known medically, as a traumatic brain aneurysm. So far it is intact, but it could leak or rupture at any time, or it could stay where it is for an indefinite period."

"Do what has to be done now, Doctor Panje! Why hasn't treatment already started?"

"There are a few papers for you to sign since you are her guardian as well as her fiancé. These are for permission to perform more exploratory procedures immediately and to follow up with surgery, if required. She opened the folder she carried, took out some forms and handed them and a pen to Yasin, pointing to where his signature was needed. He took the folder from her and signed each one with a shaky hand. As soon as he finished, Doctor Panje said, "Now we'll start everything moving."

As they left the lobby and walked together down the corridor towards Laila's room, Yasin asked, "Why did you not call me at once? You may have lost valuable time!"

"The results of a particular test I called for were just given to me a few minutes before I saw you. I phoned you when I got them. You were probably on your way here. I was just going to try again, but by chance, we met. In an emergency situation, the hospital administrator has the jurisdiction to provide consent. So even without your signature, Laila would have whatever surgery might be necessary."

Unlike his usual calm demeanor, Yasin held his hands to his head, desperately trying to cover the tears welling in his eyes.

"Her fall brought Laila here. Now that the aneurysm has been discovered, we have the opportunity to stop its destructive path." She looked at Yasin pityingly as she'd looked at so many whose loved ones were stricken with life-threatening test results. "Did Laila ever complain of headaches, nausea, vomiting or have periods of loss of consciousness?"

Yasin took his hands from his face and said, "None of those, Doctor. Laila rarely complained."

"Please, Mr. Adeeb—go meet with Laila now, and you alone can decide how much to tell her at this point."

Yasin straightened up, seemingly regaining his composure, and said, "Thank you for being honest with me. I am overwhelmed, but I have trust in you, Doctor Panje."

"We'll do everything we can," she said. "If you have any questions, I can be contacted here. Leave a message and I'll get back to you as soon as possible. Doctor Panje looked directly at Yasin as she spoke and thought—this man is truly concerned but I see more in his face. After living in India, England and the United States, she'd met many people—some who were kind and helpful and others who were dangerous. This man is not only troubled—he is trouble!"

With a sigh, she added, "Sorry, I must go now."

"Of course, I understand."

They walked off in opposite directions, Doctor Panje pausing only to answer her pager. After learning why she was urgently wanted, the doctor made a quick about-face. Running back down the hallway, she quickly caught up with Yasin shouting, "Something's happened to Laila. Hurry! By then they were only a few feet from her room, where a crowd was already forming.

33

Delray Beach and Boca Raton, Florida

When Yasin and Doctor Panje breathlessly entered Laila's room, it was so crowded they could barely push their way in. Surrounding her were a crash cart, an EKG machine, a ventilator, a doctor, the floor RN and a medical technician. Laila lay lifeless on the bed, looking as beautiful in death as she did alive. A sheet was not yet pulled over her body.

"I'm so sorry, Mr. Adeeb," Doctor Panje said, putting her hand on Yasin's shoulder. There was no reaction.

"Mr. Adeeb, are you all right?"

"You need not concern yourself about me, Doctor," Yasin said softly.

A cardiologist, checking on his patient in the next room, had been summoned and had pronounced Laila dead moments before they walked in. Doctor Panje knew that everything had been tried including CPR and CRR. Most likely the aneurysm had ruptured; Laila went into a coma and died seconds later. Of course, an autopsy would be required for confirmation.

Doctor Panje looked closely at Yasin. He was standing and staring at Laila as if his eyes could bring her back to life. His color was no better than hers. He stood frozen, a reaction far from what Doctor Panje imagined his would be. She thought he'd cry or even shriek or scoop Laila up in his arms, disbelieving the pronouncement of death. On the contrary, he remained staunch and silent for another few minutes, which appeared even more frightening. Then, turning to Doctor Panje, he said, "I must leave now; there are certain things I have to do. Thank you for your concern about Laila. I will be in touch with you later, Doctor, as to arrangements."

Looking like a walking corpse, Yasin left.

ဆၢ ဆၢ ဆၢ

Ten minutes after he arrived home, his cell phone rang. Sitting at his desk in a stupor, holding the phone to his ear, he heard Khaled's voice. "Yasin, we are here!"

"I am glad . . . and relieved."

Yasin decided he wasn't going to tell Khaled of Laila's death. He is the only person left that I love—love as a son born to me. Let him be saved to have the good life that Laila and I cannot, he thought.

"It took a little doing. Managed to get a passport for Jill; I had to use my own—not enough time. Sold my Lexus to a used car dealer in Boca for far less than it is worth for cash and that was resolved. Now, my car is no longer in my apartment space and that could lead people to believe that we drove and did not fly somewhere."

I chartered a Learjet that took us from a small West Palm airport directly to Tortola in less than three hours. It was quite costly but since time was important to us, it had to be done.

Additional moneys I offered the plane owners provided names other than ours for their manifest."

"You did well, Khaled, but what made you choose Tortola?"

"I remembered it from a few years ago when you and I came here on some banking business. The beauty of the island impressed me then. We are surrounded by palm trees and tropical flowers, and we look out on a welcoming beach and calm blue water. When Jill and I landed, I had a taxi take us around to the less sought-after places and discovered this small hotel with cottages on the beach. This is a more obscure area and we look forward to the slow pace. We cannot wait till you and Laila are here with us. When will that be?"

"I do not know exactly. Laila and I will leave as soon as I can resolve what I have to here."

"Yasin, the hotel is called Sunset Cove. Jill and I are in one of their simple, thatched-roof cottages on the beach."

"Sounds peaceful, my son."

"It is. There were some difficulties. Jill left a note for her grandmother that did not disclose where we are, but it impressed upon her that she was never happier than now and would be in touch again soon. Giving up her family and her country for us to be together was not easy. Yet, she has done it."

"You are a good person, Khaled; never forget that. Jill is fortunate to have you at her side. I have been equally fortunate for many years."

"I do not like how you sound, Yasin. Are you telling me everything? Is Laila home now?"

"Laila is still at the hospital but should be moved in the next few days."

"I feel something is wrong, but maybe it is because I cannot believe I am away from all those pressures. I never thought I would see this life."

"Be assured—Laila and I will be together shortly. Khaled, what must be done now is for you to find a local attorney. There will be many legalities that will necessitate the use of one."

"I am aware of that, and have been on the phone all morning. An appointment has been made for me to see a solicitor this afternoon who was highly recommended by one of our contacts in the United States."

"Good—but let me know as soon as you engage him. I must send on some important documents to you. I do not want to wait until we see each other again. Along with all the information I need, see if he has a private number. I would like that, too."

"I will do as you ask, Yasin, and you should hear from me in the next few hours. Again, I must say that my world would now be perfect if you both were here with us."

"There will come a day when we will all be together, my son."

"Is everything going along well for the completion of our business?"

"Yes, but you are not to concern yourself. I am sorry but there are matters that need my attention now. Yasin hesitated a few seconds and then said, "Remember this Khaled—always be on guard. We both know *they* will seek retaliation."

"Of course, I understand and I shall be alert."

With that, the call ended.

A half-hour later Yasin, still sitting and staring at the wall, heard the ring of his cell phone again. The voice at the other end was not one he wanted to hear. It was his main contact, the man in New York City he'd spoken to earlier.

"I called to confirm that the date of our business arrangement is set for next Friday and you advised me to come out next Thursday. Of course; my assistant and I must be there the day before. Is that what you told me?"

"Yes. You are correct. And everything is still going according to plan, but we are in the process of reviewing every minute of our operation with each man."

"I can understand that. But since the date of completion is only a few days away, I prefer coming earlier. I want to speak with you in person along with your assistant Khaled. This is the biggest venture you have undertaken for our firm. Please do not be offended. But I would like to check that you both are doing your assignments perfectly."

"We cannot do that. Khaled is at the house going over every requirement with the men today, and then we both have to correct any errors we uncover in the next few days.

Unfortunately, as much as I would like to see you, we are unable to change our schedule."

"You have never failed me, Yasin, in all the years you and your business associates have worked for us. So I will have to assume you will carry out this job in the same efficient manner. Upon satisfactory completion, your funds will be transferred immediately to the accounts you submitted."

"Thank you. I must go."

"That you must."

The man from New York snapped his cell phone shut and called in his associate. "Get the contact number at that house in Wellington. I feel uneasy about Yasin. This is the first time I have ever distrusted him, so I am forced to verify his actions. I believe the young man in charge at the house is called Awad al Barrak. I have heard a few people speak of him. He may be someone worth watching for the future. But for now he must be questioned."

Along with his many other positions, Awad al Barrak's job at the Wellington house was to take all the calls. He always carried his cell phone with him. Only when he was in the water—practicing for the big moment—did the cell go unanswered. When his phone rang this time, he was watching TV news on the large-screened set the den. Most of the other young men were outside in the pool; he was alone.

The man in New York City, who'd spoken to Yasin, asked, "You are Awad al Barrak?"

"Yes."

Awad had been instructed by Yasin that anyone who phoned him on this line was part of the major plan and that he was to answer immediately and truthfully.

"I have heard many good things about you and your strong leadership abilities."

"Who is this?"

"It is not necessary for you to know my name."

"Yes, sir."

I have a question for you, young man. I understand that you and the other chosen men have been practicing for the upcoming task on a daily basis."

"Yes, sir."

"Is the assistant to Mr. Adeeb—Khaled—working with you now?"

"No sir, I have not seen Khaled or Mr. Adeeb for a few days."

"You have not?"

"No, sir."

"That is all I wanted to know. Say nothing of our conversation to anyone."

"You have my word."

"Awad al Barrak, I look forward to meeting you one day."

"I hope that day will be soon."

"Perhaps it will."

The click came immediately and left Awad looking puzzled.

Back in New York City, the caller said to his assistant, "I knew something was not right. I could tell from the way Yasin was answering. This is quite serious. I must contact the Interior Minister. After all the faith he had in this man, he will be shocked and furious. Cancel the airline reservations for Thursday. Get us on an earlier plane to West Palm Beach— make it tomorrow morning, but not too early. I am sure I will be up most of the night constructing a plan to take care of Yasin Adeeb, but not before he fulfills his obligation."

34

Delray Beach and
West Palm Beach, Florida

"Oh, baby, don't stop. Keep going. Oh, that's so good."

At that second, the phone rang in Theresa's bedroom. She was at the foot of the bed and had to lean far over to get it from the night table, her mouth wet against the receiver.

"Why the hell do you have to answer that?" Antoine said.

"Shhh. I thought it was Christy . . . maybe something happened."

Antoine flashed his winning actor's smile and said, "Now everything that was up is down—and the gal who was down is up—and on the phone."

"It's Rosie, she's crying! It's got to be important," Theresa whispered, holding her hand over the mouthpiece. Minutes went by with Theresa listening and mouthing, "Wait!" to Antoine.

"You called the police? Pull yourself together for a moment. I want to help you, but I can't understand what you're saying." Sitting up, Antoine put his arm around Theresa's shoulder, pulling her to him, trying to hear what Rosie was saying.

"Of course, we'll take you. Yes, Antoine is with me. We'll get to you within the hour, or as soon as we can. Listen to me and take something to calm you down—right now!" Theresa hung up and looked at Antoine, dazed.

"Tell me everything," he said, taking Theresa in his arms, thinking of the terrific blowjob he was getting before her nutty friend called.

"Rosie phoned the cops because Augie wasn't home by noon today. He always called her if he was staying away for the night. She said that's the only dependable thing he ever did. Rosie tried his cell, but he never answered. She left messages. As a result she wanted to report him missing so the cops would check the hospitals—maybe for a car accident. Rosie did mention that Mario might have been with Augie, and she gave descriptions of them both, along with Augie's Caddy. Just now a Detective Hendrick or Henderson phoned her and said that bodies of the men she described were found by a security guard on a construction site in West Palm—near CityPlace."

"Theresa, take it easy, it still might not be them!"

"We're going to find out because Rosie has to go to the place where they're being held for identification. Antoine, she's falling apart!" Tears streamed down Theresa's face.

"What makes you so convinced it is Augie and Mario?"

"The police think it's them! And Rosie knew Augie was going out to dinner with Mario last night to discuss business. He'd told her that. Antoine, if one body is Augie, I know the other is Mario; I feel it in my heart."

"Come on, baby, let's shower and dress and get on this thing. Don't fall apart on me, too."

Theresa continued sitting on the bed, staring into space. She reflected on most everything that had happened in her marriage: I was terrified of Mario—I hated him. I didn't have one decent day in my life with him. The only good thing that happened between us was Christy.

Antoine took her face in his hands and said, "Honey, don't you see, if the other guy turns out to be Mario, it'll be better for us . . . and Christy too. We'll be a family."

Theresa looked at him and said nothing. Thoughts shot through her mind like bullets. For over two years, I've been on my own—just Christy and me—and by my working for Nuri, we've survived. I was making money—doing well, at least until these horrible things started happening. I love Antoine, but do I really want to marry him, or do I want to keep my independence?

𝔰𝔬𝔠𝔰 𝔰𝔬𝔠𝔰 𝔰𝔬𝔠𝔰

When Theresa and Antoine arrived at Rosie's condo, she was on the phone, her hands shaking as she spoke to her daughter. Georgiana and Christy were at a friend's birthday barbeque in the same development and weren't expected to return home until about ten that evening.

"Wanted you to know that I'm going to spend a few hours with Theresa and Antoine, sweetie. Okay—go back to your friends. Enjoy yourselves. I should be home by the time you both get back here. Love you too, Georgiana."

After Rosie hung up, she looked at Theresa and said, "If it is Augie, I don't know how I'll tell her. He wasn't the best father, but she loved him."

"Let's wait and see. There's no point in saying anything now."

"You're right, Theresa. I thank you both so much for coming," Rosie said with tears flowing from her red-rimmed eyes as Theresa hugged her tightly. A few minutes later they left the apartment and walked towards Antoine's car.

Driving in silence, they reached the West Palm Beach construction site in about forty minutes. There was a crowd gathered, a number of Sheriff's Deputies, cruisers, and the yellow CRIME SCENE DO NOT ENTER tape cordoning off the area. It was the only thing that kept the onlookers from going and viewing the bodies themselves.

Spotting a tall man in a suit, shirt and tie, badge affixed, the three headed his way. "Detective Hendrick?" Rosie asked.

"Yes, and you are?"

"I'm Rosie Costellano. You asked me to come here. These are my friends, Theresa Giamonte and Antoine Boyce. Theresa Giamonte is possibly the wife of the other man found."

He nodded to them all, dispensing with the hand shaking, and gave Antoine a look he'd received many times before when he was with Theresa.

"The bodies were brought up from an area where they were discovered and are being held at the back of this site. There were no valuables or any identification found on either of these men. It appears that the killer or killers took whatever they had with them. Follow me, please, and if you identify them as your husbands, be prepared. Their appearances have been changed somewhat due to the injuries that were inflicted."

"We're okay," Rosie said, softly. Antoine stared at her—then caught Theresa's eye, letting her know he was ready to respond to what might happen next.

There was a van not far off with two men, wearing I.D.'s, leaning against it, smoking. Noticing his trio looking that way, Detective Hendrick motioned towards the two men explaining, "They're from the Removal Service of the Medical Examiner's Office in West Palm Beach, basically the Morgue. We're all waiting for the Medical Examiner, who just called to say that something had come up, but he'll be here shortly."

Their eyes never left the Detective's face.

"Do you have any questions now?"

"No," they said in unison.

"Those men are waiting for us to release the bodies. We'll do that as soon as you confirm or deny their identities as your husbands. After the Medical Examiner does his job, he'll sign off the necessary papers for their removal to the Morgue. The Sheriff's Office has completed a primary investigation of the area where the men were located. They took what evidence they found before bringing them here."

Rosie, Theresa and Antoine followed Detective Hendrick to where the hastily collected, soiled construction tarps covered the men. He removed the coverings leaving the bodies exposed—their heads battered and bloody. Both women looked intently at the pair. Rosie immediately screamed, "Augie! Augie!" then collapsed. Antoine, anxiously watching for the women's reactions, caught and held Rosie before she hit the ground.

Theresa stood unresponsive, but said softly, "Yes, that is my husband, Mario."

35

Boca Raton, Florida

At the close of the phone conversation with his New York City contact, Yasin sensed the man no longer trusted him. And for all these years, his intuition had been right. As a result, Yasin's most important concern was keeping Khaled and his girlfriend safe. The contact was advised to fly in next Thursday. What Yasin needed now was a strong diversion plus destroying as much as possible of anything that connected Khaled to the organization. It took only about a half-hour of figuring every angle until he called the cell phone for the Wellington house, which was answered on the first ring.

"Yes?"

"Awad, this is Yasin. Are you all set to go?"

"We are, as I told you before. We wait for your word."

"This is it. Have the teams at their assigned bridges tonight. I assume you have varying times for them to leave depending upon the distance they each have to travel."

"Yes, Sir."

"I want the action set to go off at 8 tomorrow morning."

"It will be done."

"Each team is to return to the house once its mission is completed. I will be there about 5 AM. —probably well before. I will have your payments, last minute instructions, along with all the documents that you will need. Remember, no one leaves the house, even for a few minutes, once he has returned. There will be enough time before 8 AM for the men to drive to their next assignment."

"Of course, Yasin. We are all looking forward to completing this job . . . and then on to the next."

"Fine. I leave this most important directive in your hands. Awad, nothing must go wrong."

"Nothing will."

"Just to be sure, go over the list of Intracoastal bridges again with the group. Review the individual orders from the first to the last."

"I will see that this is taken care of."

"Good."

Yasin realized he would need strong coffee and a couple of shots of Scotch to get him through this day. Taking the bottle from his desk drawer, he uncapped it and drank until his body felt completely warm. Getting up to make coffee seemed like a heavy task—but nothing at all compared to what he planned for the next few hours.

His eyes went to the newspaper he'd left on the kitchen table. As he filled the pot with water, he noticed a headline: *Chase Ends in Capture of Murder Suspects.* Skimming the article just to get his mind off his own problems, he picked up the lines about the discovery of two, terribly brutalized dead men in a West Palm Beach construction site. *Identification of the bodies was not yet released. A suspect drove the Cadillac belonging to one of the deceased men. The speeding car was ditched on the Turnpike minutes before Deputies of the Palm Beach County Sheriff's Office apprehended them. The two suspects were being held without bail at the Palm Beach County Jail on suspicion of murder.*

Waiting for the coffee to finish perking, he continued reading. *The Sheriff's Office reported the suspects might be part of a local gang currently stealing cars in senior communities. Anthony Hodges, 19, and Jamal Miley, 18, after having their rights read—*

told the Deputies they would not say anything else until they were given a lawyer.

Those bastards, Yasin thought. What a country! Criminals are familiar with the law because they have been so often arrested. Now, they are the ones to make demands. The story continued: *One of the two Deputies on the car chase had pulled over when he noticed a figure stumbling on the roadside, covered in mud. Hardly able to speak, Sharim Williams, 18, was taken to St. Mary's Medical Center and reported in stable condition. Considered a possible third suspect, he will be questioned further when able to respond. All suspects live near each other in Pleasant City, a neighborhood in West Palm Beach.*

Yasin dropped the paper, a look of disgust on his face, and returned to his desk. Will the violence and brutality ever stop? He acknowledged to himself that he had been responsible for much of what he now despised. Yasin grabbed a pad and pen and started writing in sequence what must be done. He knew he must end his self-hatred and focus only on protecting Khaled and Jill. There were many decisions to be made and any slip-up now and the chance of saving them would be gone.

℘)℃   ℘)℃   ℘)℃

An hour passed and Yasin was so involved with his notations that his cell phone rang several times before he answered. It was Khaled.

"I just left the attorney's office, engaged him and made all the arrangements we need for now. He appears to be the man we want. He does not ask too many questions and is available to do whatever asked . . . for a price, of course. Should we need witnesses' signatures, they will appear, as well as any additional agreements required which may be unknown to us at this time."

"That is perfect. Do not concern yourself about money now, my son. It is more important that that all these legal issues get resolved."

"They will be, Yasin. I assure you."

The phone on his desk rang. Caller I.D. showed it was Doctor Panje; this was her second call today. I know she will offer her condolences again but for her it is more important to ask me about the funeral arrangements, he thought. Laila was still in the hospital morgue. Yasin let it ring, having already shut off the message machine.

He kept up his conversation with Khaled, though knowing if he continued, somehow Khaled would again suspect that something was wrong—very wrong. This is what he must avoid, and with that in mind, said, "Khaled, the pressure is on now. I must go—I no longer have you to help me, and it is not easy."

"Of course. I only want to give you the details you need to contact this lawyer. He was informed that you are my partner and will be corresponding with him by fax. He is totally agreeable."

"Thank you," Yasin said, as he listened and made note of the particulars.

"You will be hearing from me shortly, Khaled. Meanwhile, you and Jill enjoy each day," he said, snapping the phone shut.

Yasin tore the pages from his pad and put them aside. Once written, his mind retained them. He took pen in hand and pulled some heavily engraved letterheads from a drawer. The lawyer's name, address and fax number went on a cover sheet. The gist of his letter was that he was granting a Power-of-Attorney to Khaled to be responsible for any and all legal commitments where Yasin's name was invoked. A copy of his Will was also to be included, naming Khaled as his beneficiary and Executor. Listed, too, were bank accounts in the Cayman Islands by their account number and password. The top of his desk was piled high with forms and letters regarding properties and businesses.

He continued on until the work was completed and then faxed all he thought necessary to the attorney. Confirmation of receipt came through immediately. The agreement with the attorney's signature followed shortly afterward.

Removing the high security, crosscut, paper shredder from his office closet, Yasin shredded all letters, forms and agreements that were in his files, including current memos.

This drastic change in his plans came after Laila's death. He realized *she* was his reason to live and without her there was none. Plus, the continuous murders—the violence—sickened him now, even though it had been so much a part of his life. Unfortunately, to end it, more destruction must be used, he thought sadly. After accepting that fact, he felt a sense of relief and exhilaration.

Glancing at his watch, Yasin walked over to the bedroom, heading for his closet. Pulling up part of the carpeting installed on the closet floor, he exposed a buried safe. He worked the combination and then opened it. There was no cash, fine jewelry or loose diamonds—it was entirely filled with highly-sophisticated, lightweight and deadly plastic explosives.

36

Wellington, Florida

Awad al Barak had proven himself a born military leader, strong and intelligent. He kept his men focused on their duties so they were loyal without his having to be constantly demanding their commitment. Awad was also quick to give praise when deserved, and thereby gained their allegiance. After his last words with Yasin on the phone, he thought about the private conversation they had several weeks before at the house. Awad respected the man and felt that Yasin returned that respect. He had felt free to ask a question of Yasin about something that plagued him since he and the team were organized and he had been informed of the mission.

"Why are we blowing up insignificant, Intracoastal bridges in Florida? Far more damage—more impact—could be achieved if our explosive team blew up huge ports, railroads or even power plants. Why were these small bridges chosen?"

Yasin had looked at him with a pleased expression and said, "You are curious and analytical my boy, and those are good traits. Awad, this decision was long in the making. The places you propose may appear more logical, but our purpose is to frighten Americans, not only in Florida but also in every state. Once these targeted bridges blow, resulting in panic from fires and loss of life, average working people will never know if the simple routes to their jobs are safe."

"Besides destroying peace of mind, there will be extreme disruptions of car, truck, and water traffic. We have chosen twelve young men, plus you as their leader. They have been trained to swim under water and set explosives expertly. You will choose which two-man team to join. I am sure you are familiar with the targeted Intracoastal bridges.

"Of course, I see them before me in my sleep."

"These six bridges were chosen because they span a distance across the southeastern coast of Florida and their security is not as strong as other Intracoastal bridges."

"I understand, Yasin."

Without a pause, Yasin continued, "Mainly, we want to instill apprehension—a feeling of impending terror—that is what our organization wants. We were hired for this purpose. Our employer wants the population to feel that their government cannot protect them, and that they do not know where we will strike next, and we will—the targets are already on paper. It does not matter, Awad, that we could create more death and destruction; we will have created anxiety and put fear in the minds of every person in this country."

Awad absorbed every word Yasin spoke. He'd admired him even more and knew their plan would work, provided all went well—and why shouldn't it? Awad had taken care of every detail. His men practiced their scuba diving constantly; they were like fish in the water. They were familiar with the security of the designated sites and expert in their individual explosive responsibilities. Awad believed that after this, new doors of opportunity would open for him and his crew.

Living in the United States, however, where there were no burqas covering women's bodies and no scarves on their heads, Awad and his men were constantly enticed. Burqas and head coverings could be seen in Muslim enclaves; those were places he and his men didn't frequent. Awad wanted to make love to every scantily dressed, young American woman he saw and to own every sleek sports car that caught his eye. But he set the pace for his crew and knew the job came first and that they must keep a low profile. In setting explosives or leading his team safely, no one was more serious, clever or efficient than Awad. Knowing this led him to believe that one day he'd have it all.

During their personal conversation, Awad recalled that minutes before Yasin left, he'd said, "I am sure you are aware that you and your associates are an unusual group. You are mercenaries—trained superbly by the best instructors in the Middle East. You were all investigated, interviewed and then each selected carefully. As mercenaries, we all work for the highest bidder. But, you, Awad, and your team, by excelling in this task, will be recognized for your success. The rewards for your risks are great. Personal or religious feelings have nothing to do with our jobs. We are all unique in seeking life—not death for ourselves—and all the wealth and happiness it brings. *This* is our cause!"

Awad had smiled and nodded in agreement.

ᔕᘉᏡ   ᔕᘉᏡ   ᔕᘉᏡ

Noticing the time, Awad realized there was much yet he had to oversee before their mission began. Everything in the house was to be ready for a prompt departure, but his mind kept replaying Yasin's remarks about being mercenaries.

Awad would have been shocked if he knew of Laila's sudden death, and even more so how it would drastically affect his own life. He'd first met her when she accompanied Yasin and Khaled on a visit to Wellington. She was introduced as Yasin's fiancée. Awad was completely overwhelmed by her beauty, as were the other young men. Realizing how they all reacted and aware of Yasin's high position in the organization, he had advised his team strongly, "This woman is Yasin's fiancée." He'd added, "Laila is not to be stared at if she visits here again, and not even her name is to be spoken among us in conversation. She could be trouble—understand me—it is not worth it!"

The most important thing now, he thought, was to stop looking back, and to call the men together and give them their final instructions. He planned to speak in both English and Arabic so there would be no misunderstanding. Awad was prepared and anxious to begin the job. Confident of the outcome, he knew nothing of what lay ahead for his team and him. Awad would never have thought that this was his last day as their leader.

37

*Boca Raton, Delray Beach
and Wellington, Florida*

When Yasin set explosives, his hands had the sensitivity of a concert violinist holding his bow, ready to play. But what he produced was an unthinkable disaster—not a concert masterpiece. Prior to becoming a highly paid organizer of mercenaries, he was an explosives expert trained on all types in Pakistan. Yasin developed an ability to both create and to disarm them. This combat demolition training helped make him a rich man. He'd taught Khaled all he knew, and they both were responsible for many targeted buildings in cities in the Middle East, Europe, Africa and South America.

Back at the apartment, Yasin knew there was little time left for what he recently decided to do. Quickly, yet carefully, he prepared the C-4 plastic explosives. They were in brick form, easy to mold, and they looked more like bread dough than something deadly. Planting the two bombs would be easy in comparison to the embassies, synagogues, luxury hotels and tourist spots he and Khaled once tackled. He removed only the explosives, timing devices and detonators needed for the project. The safe was impenetrable after it was locked.

Requiring something to carry his materials, Yasin headed for Laila's closet, thinking her gym bag would do. His eyes caught the gold-framed photo of her on his night table. It had been taken the day he and Khaled took Laila with them to the Wellington house. She looked so beautiful then that he insisted on capturing her on his camera. He knew the young men there possessed Laila with their eyes. Their envy of him was obvious.

Sitting on the soft, satin sheet of the not-slept-in bed, he held the photo in his hand and whispered, "Laila, my love, you are gone." He continued to stare at her likeness as if he held her in his arms. "I did not know how much I loved you until I lost you," he said aloud as he laid the photograph down gently.

For a moment he thought of his neglect in not making funeral arrangements for her. Also, there was the money due the hospital. He thought of Doctor Panje's kindness, but still she and all the other doctors were not able to save his Laila from death. Fuck her and the hospital! With all their modern technology, how could they let Laila die? He'd give them nothing. They deserved nothing, and what would a proper burial do for Laila or for himself, he thought.

Waiting the few hours until he could set the three bombs was difficult, but he was unable to leave until it was dark. Then the beauty salon area would be almost deserted, Nuri and his family should be sleeping and the Wellington house would be vacant. Meanwhile, he went through all his files and drawers again, making sure there was nothing left to trace. The only concern Yasin had was to keep Khaled and Jill alive, which meant having their whereabouts unknown. This required eliminating people who could identify Khaled, plus every piece of paper that involved him. Yasin didn't include those people he felt were too fearful to speak like Nuri's employees; they knew better than to come forward. And tonight the problem of Nuri and his family would be resolved, too.

Though he hadn't eaten all day, Yasin felt no hunger, but he also knew he couldn't take a chance of losing his focus when he'd need it most. He poured a cup of coffee from his pot of strong Colombian and tore open a fresh package of dates.

Several hours later, dressed in black, carrying his .45 in a slim, unseen holster under his zippered jacket, he left the building. As the valet drove his car up to him, Yasin went around to the passenger side, opened the door, placing the gym bag carefully on the seat. "Thank you, Jeff. I know it is late," Yasin said, smiling at the young man, and putting a folded twenty-dollar bill in his hand.

"No problem, Mr. Adeeb. When I'm here, anytime is fine."

Yasin pulled out of the garage slowly, headed for his first stop—Nuri's beauty salon. As he drove, he convinced himself again that there was no brutality in causing the deaths of Nuri, his wife and daughter. If he did not take this action, he knew they would be killed by the organization in a torturous manner—one that made his way, humane.

He'd forgotten that a small nightclub had taken over two of the empty stores in the strip mall recently. There were plenty of cars coming and going and parked in the lot. The hard rock music filtered out—in earshot of the entire area. His was just one among the many cars, pick-up trucks and SUV's.

He climbed out of his car and walked towards the new salon construction, seeking the best spot for the explosive. It was a night with just a few stars, making it more to his benefit. A convertible carrying several young men drove passed Yasin. They were all drinking beer and laughing. Suddenly the driver screeched to a stop and one of them called out to him, "Hey! The hotties in that club are way too young for you, old man."

"Thank you for the advice," he said warmly, automatically touching his weapon, but kept walking, wanting no further discussion.

The action was at the club, and Yasin thought no one would notice him or what he was doing. Knowing he was armed and ready, he still kept his eyes open for anyone else who might approach and cause trouble. He made sure the car filled with those spoiled-rotten, drunk Americans was parked and they all were in the club before taking out the materials. Yasin attached the detonator along with the timing device set to go off at 3:45 AM. This would result in a number of police, fire and rescue vehicles converging on the area, leaving very few to respond to what lay ahead for them at 4 AM, 5 AM and 8 AM.

Nuri also lived in Delray Beach—north of Atlantic Avenue, in a small ranch house with an attached garage on a street—one block long. It took Yasin less than fifteen minutes to get there. This was not a gated or guarded community; he parked a block away. There was not a person on the street and Yasin, carrying the small gym bag, walked quickly towards Nuri's house. Located in a working class neighborhood, it was not surprising that this late there was little traffic and no one around. He knew that Nuri had no alarm system because he'd heard him speaking about looking into getting one for his home and the new salon. Yasin continued to the side of the garage, putting his bag on the ground carefully. Opening it, he removed the small sticky bomb and attached it to the garage wall; setting the timing device to go off at 4 AM. The explosion would ignite Nuri's car immediately and the flames should go right through the house in no time. Zipping up the now lighter bag, he took it in hand and walked briskly back to his car. Now, that was good fortune—not even a barking dog, he thought. Yasin opened and closed the car door quietly, put his bag on the passenger seat, started the engine and headed west.

There was more than enough time to get to the house in Wellington. When he reached it, the young men would have already left for their assignments. With the little traffic he encountered, Yasin managed to get there in about forty-five minutes. The house was still; the surrounding areas were equally silent. Homes here were acres apart. He parked his car in the back, away from the road, and slung the bag over his shoulder. Finding the right area to attach the bomb took a little time. He decided on the wall, opposite the pool, leading to the den where the men usually gathered. But it really made no difference since this bomb was so intense, the entire house and much of the surroundings would be destroyed.

It took Yasin a little longer for installation than the last two, perhaps because his hands were now shaking. Setting the explosion for 5:00 AM, he walked to his car, the empty bag in his hand. He'd told Adwar to be back by that time, so he was certain they would all have returned. They wanted their money and their instructions. More importantly, they wanted to be out of there and well on their way to their next assignment when the bridges blew. Yasin made it back to his apartment in record time.

$\wp\wp$ $\wp\wp$ $\wp\wp$

Sitting at his desk at 3:45 AM, Yasin heard the explosion— and felt it. Nuri's salon in Delray Beach was only a few miles away. Sounds of sirens responding were quick. Another explosion was heard around 4 AM. After the first summons, the near-by firehouse had their trucks and volunteer firefighters at Nuri's home within minutes. They were battling the intense blaze when one of them heard ringing.

Nuri had set his old alarm clock for 4:15 AM. When he'd returned home earlier, too upset and exhausted to drive, he convinced himself that all he needed was a few hours' sleep and they'd leave before sunrise. That fucking bastard, Yasin, believed he was staying another week anyway so why risk an accident? I've got to be sensible, he'd thought. The family was sleeping when the bomb went off.

Asphyxiated by the heavy smoke, they were all dead when the firemen reached them.

$\wp\wp$ $\wp\wp$ $\wp\wp$

An hour later Yasin was still seated like a statue, holding a cup of cold coffee. Straining, he thought he could make out what sounded like a muffled blast. Most people, he was sure, would think it was a clap of thunder, but he was positive it was the Wellington house going up in flames, killing all its inhabitants.

Now everything was done except for the real targets the organization had chosen. A sweat formed on Yasin's head, going on to cover his entire body. He knew they wouldn't pay him, and they wouldn't let him live either—no matter how effective the loss of the bridges was. He'd lied to them. Although this was the first time he had, it made no difference. Yasin continued sitting in his office, staring into space, for yet another hour.

Then suddenly, eyes bulging, face red, and every vein in his neck standing out, he shouted, "Laila! Without you I cannot go on. Kahled and I realized what was important in our lives— only too late—at least too late for us, my darling." His mind raced. Perhaps Khaled and Jill would still have a chance. There was no reason now for more killings and destruction for the sake of an organization that had no respect for life. Money was its God. And to think, once I saw nothing wrong with that.

Yasin shook his head and put his face in his hands. When he took his hands away, he was smiling. This is a laugh—a fucking laugh. One day, as impossible as it may seem, he thought, I may be regarded as a hero. By destroying this team of mercenaries, much damage will be done to the organization and their future plans. There will be people still living, who would have been killed if the organization's present and projected attacks were not stopped. In the end, it will have no affect on me, he thought. Yasin reached for the phone on his desk, stared at it with an expression of amazement, paused, and then punched in 9-1-1.

The call was answered quickly.

"9-1-1. Where is your emergency?"

"At 8 o'clock this morning explosives are set to go off under some Intracoastal bridges. They are: McCormick—US 90 in Jacksonville, Main Street in Daytona Beach, SR A1A in Ft.

Pierce, SR 802 in Lake Worth, Oakland Park Blvd. in Ft. Lauderdale, and Sunny Isles in North Miami. Each has a sticky bomb attached to the north-side span, underneath the bridge."

"What is your problem, Sir? Tell me again—exactly what is happening?"

Yasin shouted—with the determination and the strength of a field commander, "I AM REPORTING EXPLOSIVES SET TO GO OFF AT DESIGNATED INTRACOASTAL BRIDGES FROM JACKSONVILLE TO MIAMI. I HAVE ALREADY NAMED THEM—AND THEIR LOCATIONS!"

"Who is involved?"

"Let me speak. You do not have much time to stop their plan. I will hang up as soon as I have finished. Do not waste a moment tracing this call. You must contact whoever can authorize explosive-removal teams to go to every one of those bridges I gave to you. If this is not done immediately, you will be responsible for losing the opportunity to save lives as well as the needless destruction of infrastructure and property."

"Sir . . . sir . . . sir . . ."

Yasin cut the connection, pulled the pistol from its holster and without hesitation put it into his mouth and pulled the trigger. A trail of blood trickled down his body onto the fine Persian carpet as his last legacy.

38

Tortola (The British Virgin Islands)

Four Years Later

Awad al Barak swatted a bloodthirsty mosquito on his nose and cursed in Arabic at his luck. He sat uncomfortably in what looked like a native fishing boat, but strangely enough it was equipped with a swift Yamaha, 75 HP outboard motor. Dangling a line in the water gave him too much time to think. His dark skin, torn shirt and faded, old fishing hat disguised him perfectly. Awad's mind drifted to that night of the explosion at the Wellington house.

စာလ   စာလ   စာလ

He was outside, retrieving the cell phone he'd left in his car, even though he'd been ordered not to leave the house once he returned. He knew if there was no response to an important call that came in, he'd be in big trouble. Left with no other choice, he had dashed out to his car parked in the grass at the end of the driveway.

As Awad picked up the phone lying on the seat, an earth-shaking explosion erupted, immediately setting the house aflame. The intensity of the blast knocked him to the ground. He remembered hearing the screams of the men inside, but he could do nothing. He lay there semi-conscious for a while. When his head cleared, he touched the cuts and bruises on his body. Wiping away the blood on his face with his shirt sleeve, he thought the fact that he was alive was a miracle. Realizing he had to get out of there, he looked around, figuring the woods behind the stables would be safe, at least for a while.

Awad would never forget the tremendous flames coming from the house and those pleas for help. His position, hidden by the trees, still allowed him to see the surroundings. But staying there kept him from being discovered by the arriving fire fighters and EMS units. After he felt more alert, he walked further into the woods. Awad couldn't believe he'd been saved from certain death. Perhaps Allah had more in mind for him. Entirely godless, he was frightened by the thought. Still in shock, he waited for more light to use the phone clutched in his hand. Awad had been told to memorize a particular number at the start of the assignment and to use it only in an emergency. It could not be worse than this, he thought, as he punched in the number, thankful he remembered it.

"What the fuck happened?" he asked the man who answered.

He received no reply, but instead was asked questions to confirm his identity. Awad was also asked what he knew about earlier explosions in Delray Beach at the beauty salon and spa construction site and another at the beauty salon owner's home. Holding his head with his other hand, he had said, "I know nothing about them. It comes as another surprise to me."

The unidentified man then informed him that the organization was now searching for answers, and they would get them. "We always do," he had said. The respondent then asked Awad to pinpoint where he was and assured him that he would be picked up shortly. Many hours, it seemed to Awad, went by before two men came for him.

Awad thought back to his rescue. Rescued? Perhaps, that was the wrong word. Made into their personal hit man, might be better. He was the only one of the team to survive, the only one left to be blamed, and blame they did, along with hours of interrogation. Even when they learned that Yasin, perhaps with help from the long-gone Khaled, had caused their plan to fail, it did not stop their harassment of him. Awad kept hearing the words of the organization's top man, "We should not have saved you—we should have executed you."

He was also told that upon learning of the mission's failure, an important Interior Minister in Iraq, who was responsible for much of the plan, suffered a fatal heart attack. But regardless of how they condemned him, Awad knew his killing skills were needed. Of all the men he was forced to eliminate, not one shot of his had missed. The newly installed engine on this crude little boat would take him miles away in minutes once this job was done. And no doubt, there would be another assignment waiting.

Awad thought about the past four years and how money now meant little to him. The organization paid him well, as promised. He had a magnificent condo in Fort Lauderdale, facing the ocean, complete with a wrap-around balcony that so impressed the women he brought there. There was no shortage of them, but he longed for a normal life without the extravagances, but with family and friends—ones you could trust. Awad knew that could never be and often thought he might have been better off had he died with his men.

He had never balked at killing others. But his new instructions were clear, "You are to make sure Khaled and his family are at home, and then you are to kill Khaled's two children first, his wife next. When Khaled hears their cries and runs to them, he is to be shot dead. But you must be certain he has seen all the bodies. It has taken us years and much expense to find him on that miserable island. And, if it were not for his money-hungry lawyer who informed us of his whereabouts, we still would be looking for him and that whore of his. Awad, you know he must pay for what Yasin and he did. Khaled and his family will be used as an example so that there will be no others in our ranks to ever try anything like that again. It is a fitting punishment."

"I am aware of that," Awad had replied.

The sweat now covering his entire body was not from the sun beating down on him. He'd never killed a woman, and certainly never children. He knew he had no recourse; he and his entire family would be hunted down and slaughtered if he didn't obey.

ᔆᓍᖇ   ᔆᓍᖇ   ᔆᓍᖇ

Khaled sat at his desk, the picture window before him, framing sunny skies, the beach and azure blue water. It provided light on the four-year old newspaper story he'd read and reread. It was from the Florida Sun Sentinel, written on that fateful day that Florida citizens feared another New York City 9/11. It was that emergency call Yasin placed that brought the plan almost complete failure.

Khaled read on: *Bomb squads, local police units and Homeland Security forces raced to six intracoastal bridges along Florida's southeastern coast. A phone call received by a local 9-1-1 operator told of targeted intracoastal bridges that had explosives set to go off at 8 AM, the height of the morning rush hour. Blowing up the bridges, vehicles and passengers on the expanses at that time would have caused loss of life, injuries to those in and around the areas, plus complete destruction of the bridges. Had all the bombs detonated simultaneously, as the terrorists planned, extreme panic would have prevailed. Targeted bridges were: McCormick—US 90 in Jacksonville, Main Street in Daytona Beach, SR A1A in Ft. Pierce, SR 802 in Lake Worth, Oakland Park Blvd. in Ft. Lauderdale, and Sunny Isles in North Miami.*

Khaled went over the story as if each time he'd find something new. There were bridges listed that couldn't be saved before the detonation, as well as names of the dead found and the injured rescued and taken to hospitals. The obvious fact that a terrorist cell existed for some time in southeast Florida and was able to set up this horrendous plan, without detection, was the cry of newspaper editorials all over the United States.

Further stories reported: *There were early morning explosions of a beauty salon as well as a spa under construction next to it, along with the home of the salon's owner. The commercial buildings were in a strip mall on Atlantic Avenue in Delray Beach. Those remaining in a nightclub located at the opposite end of the mall, safely escaped. The private home was located in a small development north of Atlantic Avenue. That explosion took the lives of the salon owner, Nuri Mustafa, his wife and young daughter. No other houses on the street were damaged. Over an hour after the explosions, an exclusive home in Wellington went up in flames following another huge blast. The home and a number of vehicles on the property were completely demolished. Remains of bodies found there were burned beyond recognition. The intensity of the explosions and resultant fires were deemed as the cause. Attempts at identification are ongoing. A connection between these events is being investigated.*

Khaled read the reports as if it were the first time he saw them: *Authorities continue to seek a tie-in between the explosions in Delray Beach and Wellington and the 9-1-1 call. An Iraqi national, Yasin Adeeb, who lived in a high-rise, sea-front condominium in Boca Raton, placed the call. Discovered by tracking the 9-1-1 message made from his phone, the subject was found dead in his apartment the next day, an apparent suicide. Mr. Adeeb had phoned 9-1-1, disclosing the plot less than two hours before the bombs were to explode. Agencies assigned to the investigations have not released any more details.*

ಹೊಂ಄   ಹೊಂ಄   ಹೊಂ಄

Khaled and Jill were the happy parents of three-year old, Farah and fifteen-month old, Laith. Yasin had made sure that money would never be a problem for them. They were living the life they'd dreamed about, although Khaled was always looking over his shoulder, remembering Yasin's warnings.

Gazing out the window, he noticed a fishing boat unusually close to shore. He then heard the children cry out. "Oh, my God! No. No," he shouted and jumped up, running towards the screen door. Seeing Jill opening it, he called, "Jill, Jill, stop!"

ಸಾಂ ಸಾಂ ಸಾಂ

Awad had seen the little boy and girl sitting in the sand, each playing with a pail and shovel outside their beach house. They had to go first. His Russian Dragunov SVD was beside him, his preferred rifle, even though some sniper experts thought it a bit crude. It was deadly and had served him well. He lifted it, took a bead on the children—aiming for their heads. First he shot the boy, and then the girl. Hearing the gunshots, Khaled's wife ran outside, and the next bullet killed her. Seconds behind Jill was Khaled, yelling and looking around wildly. Too late, my friend, Awad thought. Ignoring the unusual breeze and slight rock to the boat, he brought Khaled down with his next shot. Shoving the rifle under the tarp, he then pressed the starter, and was gone—out to sea—where a waiting yacht was anchored, ready to pick him up and then sink his boat.

If Awad had remained a few moments longer, he'd have seen Khaled crawl over to Jill's still body and kiss her lips, while blood flowed from the wound that had grazed his head.

"This cannot have happened," he cried out. Khaled banged his fists on the ground. "How could I have let them die? I loved them so."

Khaled then went over to where the children lay and cradled their blood-splattered bodies to his and wept. "I know who did this, and they will pay with far more than their lives . . . all of them!" He screamed again and again till he had no voice left.